ONE WAY
or
ANOTHER

<<< >>>

ONE WAY
or
ANOTHER

stories by
Peter Cameron

PERENNIAL LIBRARY

Harper & Row, Publishers, New York
Cambridge, Philadelphia, San Francisco, Washington
London, Mexico City, São Paulo, Singapore, Sydney

"Nuptials & Heathens" and "The Last Possible Moment" first appeared in a slightly different form and with different titles in *Mademoiselle*; "Archeology" first appeared in *Grand Street*; "Excerpts from Swan Lake" and "Freddie's Haircut" first appeared in *The Kenyon Review*; "Memorial Day," "Grounded," "Homework," "Melissa & Henry—September 10, 1983," "Fast Forward," "Fear of Math," "Jump or Dive," and "Odd Jobs" first appeared in *The New Yorker*.

The author wishes to express his thanks to the MacDowell Colony and the Trust for Public Land.

A hardcover edition of this book is published by Harper & Row, Publishers, Inc.

First PERENNIAL LIBRARY edition published 1987.

Designed by Ruth Bornschlegel

Library of Congress Cataloging-in-Publication Data

Cameron, Peter.
  One way or another.

  "Perennial Library"
  I. Title.
PS3553.A434405   1987   813'.54   85-45626
ISBN 0-06-091421-1 (pbk.)

87 88 89 90 91 MPC 10 9 8 7 6 5 4 3 2 1

for Linda Asher

Contents

ONE WAY
or
ANOTHER

‑‹‹‹ ›››‑

I am eating my grapefruit with a grapefruit spoon my mother bought last summer from a door-to-door salesman on a large three-wheeled bike. My mother and I were sitting on the front steps that day and we watched him glide down the street, into our driveway, and up our front walk. He opened his case on the handlebars, and it was full of fruit appliances: pineapple corers, melon ballers, watermelon seeders, orange-juice squeezers, and grapefruit spoons. My mother bought four of the spoons and the man pedaled himself out of our lives.

That was about a year ago. Since then a lot has changed, I think as I pry the grapefruit pulp away from the skin with the serrated edge of the spoon. Since then, my mother has remarried, my father has moved to California, and I have stopped talking. Actually, I talk quite a lot at school, but never at home. I have nothing to say to anyone here.

Across the table from me, drinking Postum, is my new stepfather. He wasn't here last year. I don't think he was anywhere last year. His name is Lonnie, and my mother met him at a Seth Speaks seminar. Seth is this guy without a body who speaks out of the mouth of this lady and tells you how to fix your life. Both Lonnie and my mother have fixed their lives. "One day at a time," my mother says every morning, smiling at Lonnie and then, less happily, at me.

Lonnie is only thirteen years older than I am; he is twenty-nine but looks about fourteen. When the three of us go out together, he is taken to be my brother.

"Listen to this," Lonnie says. Both Lonnie and my mother continue to talk to me, consult with me, and read things to me, in the hope that I will forget and speak. "If gypsy moths continue to destroy trees at their present rate, North America will become a desert incapable of supporting any life by the year 4000." Lonnie has a morbid sense of humor and delights in macabre newspaper fillers. Because he knows I won't answer, he doesn't glance up at me. He continues to stare at his paper and says, "Wow. Think of that."

I look out the window. My mother is sitting in an inflated rubber boat in the swimming pool, scrubbing the fiberglass walls with a stiff brush and Mr. Clean. They get stained during the winter. She does this every Memorial Day. We always open the pool this weekend, and she always blows up the yellow boat, puts on her Yankees hat so her hair won't turn orange, and paddles around the edge of the pool, leaving a trail of suds.

Last year, as she scrubbed, the diamond from her old engagement ring fell out and sank to the bottom of the pool. She was still married to my father, although they were planning to separate after a last "family vacation" in July. My mother shook the suds off her hand and raised it in front of her face, as if she were admiring a new ring. "Oh, Stephen!" she said. "I think I've lost my diamond."

"What?" I said. I still talked then.

"The diamond fell out of my ring. Look."

I got up from the chair I was sitting on and kneeled beside the pool. She held out her hand, the way women do in old movies when they expect it to be kissed. I looked down at her ring and she was right: the diamond was gone. The setting looked like an empty hand tightly grabbing nothing.

"Do you see it?" she asked, looking down into the pool. Because we had just taken the cover off, the water was murky. "It must be down there," she said. "Maybe if you dove in?" She looked at me with a nice, pleading look on her face. I took my shirt off. I felt her looking at my chest. There is no hair on my chest, and every time my mother sees it I know she checks to see if any has grown.

I dove into the pool. The water was so cold my head ached. I opened my eyes and swam quickly around the bottom. I felt like one of those Japanese pearl fishers. But I didn't see the diamond.

I surfaced and swam to the side. "I don't see it," I said. "I can't see anything. Where's the mask?"

"Oh, dear," my mother said. "Didn't we throw it away last year?"

"I forget," I said. I got out of the pool and stood shivering in the sun. Suddenly I got the idea that if I found the diamond maybe my parents wouldn't separate. I know it sounds ridiculous, but at that moment, standing with my arms crossed over my chest, watching my mother begin to cry in her inflatable boat—at that moment, the diamond sitting on the bottom of the pool took on a larger meaning, and I thought that if it was replaced in the tiny clutching hand of my mother's ring we might live happily ever after.

So I had my father drive me downtown, and I bought a diving mask at the five-and-ten, and when we got home I put it on—first spitting on the glass so it wouldn't fog —and dove into the water, and dove again and again, until I actually found the diamond, glittering in a mess of leaves and bloated inchworms at the bottom of the pool.

I throw my grapefruit rind away, and go outside and sit on the edge of the diving board with my feet in the water. My mother watches me for a second, probably deciding if it's worthwhile to say anything. Then she goes back to her scrubbing.

Later, I am sitting by the mailbox. Since I've stopped talking, I've written a lot of letters. I write to men in prisons, and I answer personal ads, claiming to be whatever it is the placer desires: "an elegant educated lady for afternoon pleasure," or a "GBM." The mail from prisons is the best: long letters about nothing, since it seems nothing is done in prison. A lot of remembering. A lot of bizarre requests: Send me a shoehorn. Send me an empty egg carton (arts and crafts?). Send me an electric toothbrush. I like writing letters to people I've never met.

Lonnie is planting geraniums he bought this morning in front of the A & P when he did the grocery shopping. Lonnie is very good about "doing his share." I am not about mine. Every night I wait with delicious anticipation for my mother to tell me to take out the garbage: "How many times do I have to tell you? Can't you just do it?"

Lonnie gets up and walks over to me, trowel in hand. He has on plaid Bermuda shorts and a Disney World T-shirt. If I talked, I'd ask him when he went to Disney World. But I can live without the information.

Lonnie flips the trowel at me and it slips like a knife into the ground a few inches from my leg. "Bingo!" Lonnie says. "Scare you?"

I think when a person stops talking people forget that he can still hear. Lonnie is always saying dumb things to me—things you'd only say to a deaf person or a baby.

"What a day," Lonnie says, as if to illustrate this point. He stretches out beside me, and I look at his long white legs. He has sneakers and white socks on. He never goes barefoot. He is too uptight to go barefoot. He would step on a piece of glass immediately. That is the kind of person Lonnie is.

The Captain Ice Cream truck rolls lazily down our street. Lonnie stands up and reaches in his pocket. "Would you like an ice pop?" he asks me, looking at his change.

I shake my head no. An ice pop? Where did he grow up —Kentucky?

Lonnie walks into the street and flags down the ice-cream truck as if it's not obvious what he's standing there for.

The truck slows down and the ice-cream man jumps out. It is a woman. "What can I get you?" she says, open-ing the freezer on the side of the truck. It's the old-fash-ioned kind of truck, with the ice cream hidden in its frozen depths. I always thought you needed to have in-credibly long arms to be a good Captain Ice Cream person.

"Well, I'd like a nice ice pop," Lonnie says.

"A Twin Bullet?" suggests the woman. "What flavor?"

"Do you have cherry?" Lonnie asks.

"Sure," the woman says. "Cherry, grape, orange, lemon, cola, and tutti-frutti."

For a second I have a horrible feeling that Lonnie will want a tutti-frutti. "I'll have cherry," he says.

Lonnie comes back, peeling the sticky paper from his cherry Bullet. It's a bright pink color. The truck drives away. "Guess how much this cost," Lonnie says, sitting beside me on the grass. "Sixty cents. It's a good thing you didn't want one." He licks his fingers and then the ice stick. "Do you want a bite?" He holds it out toward me.

Lonnie is so patient and so sweet. It's just too bad he's such a nerd. I take a bite of his cherry Bullet.

"Good, huh?" Lonnie says. He watches me eat for a second, then takes a bite himself. He breaks the Bullet in half and eats it in a couple of huge bites. A little pink juice runs down his chin.

"What are you waiting for?" he asks. I nod toward the mailbox.

"It's Memorial Day," Lonnie says. "The mail doesn't come." He stands up and pulls the trowel out of the ground. I think of King Arthur. "There is no mail for anyone today," Lonnie says. "No matter how long you wait." He hands me his two Bullet sticks and returns to his geraniums.

I have this feeling, holding the stained wooden sticks, that I will keep them for a long time, and come across them one day, and remember this moment, incorrectly.

After the coals in the barbecue have melted into powder, the fireflies come out. They hesitate in the air, as if stunned by dusk.

Lonnie and my mother are sitting beside the now clean pool, and I am sitting on the other side of the "natural forsythia fence" that is planted around it, watching the bats swoop from tree to tree, feeling the darkness clot all around me. I can hear Lonnie and my mother talking, but I can't make out what they are saying.

I love this time of day—early evening, early summer. It makes me want to cry. We always had a barbecue on Memorial Day with my father, and my mother cooked this year's hamburgers on her new barbecue, which Lonnie bought her for Mother's Day (she's old enough to be his mother, but she isn't, I would have said, if I talked), in the same dumb, cheerful way she cooked last year's. She has no sense of sanctity, or ritual. She would give Lonnie my father's clothes if my father had left any behind to give.

My mother walks toward me with the hose, then past me toward her garden, to spray her pea plants. "O.K.," she yells to Lonnie, who stands by the spigot. He turns the knob and then goes inside. The light in the kitchen snaps on.

My mother stands with one hand on her hip, the other raising and lowering the hose, throwing large fans of water over the garden. She used to bathe me every night, and I think of the peas hanging in their green skins, dripping. I lie with one ear on the cool grass, and I can hear the water drumming into the garden. It makes me sleepy.

Then I hear it stop, and I look up to see my mother walking toward me, the skin on her bare legs and arms glowing. She sits down beside me, and for a while she says nothing. I pretend I am asleep on the ground, although I know she knows I am awake.

Then she starts to talk, as I knew she would. My mother says, "You are breaking my heart." She says it as if it were literally true, as if her heart were actually breaking. "I just want you to know that," she says. "You're old enough to know that you are breaking my heart."

I sit up. I look at my mother's chest, as if I could see her heart breaking. She has on a polo shirt with a little blue whale on her left breast. I am afraid to look at her face.

We sit like that for a while, and darkness grows around us. When I open my mouth to speak, my mother uncoils her arm from her side and covers my mouth with her hand.

I look at her.

"Wait," she says. "Don't say anything yet."

I can feel her flesh against my lips. Her wrist smells of chlorine. The fireflies, lighting all around us, make me dizzy.

≺≺≺   **Nuptials & Heathens**   ≻≻≻

Joan is trying to decide if Tom's habit of switching the car radio from station to station is endearing or annoying. As they drive north of Boston, into the late night and away from the good stations, he punches the buttons more and more frequently. He is never satisfied with one station for long. They are driving to his parents' house in Maine for the weekend.

She rolls up her window because it is getting cold, and puts her empty Tab can on the floor at her feet, then picks it up because she's not sure it is something she should do in his car. When they stopped for gas she took fifty-five cents from the "toll money" (they were off the highway and through with tolls) and bought a Tab from the machine. When she tilted the can under Tom's chin for him to sip from, he said, "Ugh, Tab. Couldn't you have got a soda we both liked?"

Tom's mother, Mrs. Thorenson, hears them arrive, but she doesn't get out of bed. She doesn't look so great in the middle of the night, and first impressions are first impressions. She listens to them come inside, hears them trying to be quiet, hears Tom pointing things out—"There's the ocean down there. See it?" She listens to them use the bathroom. It sounds like they're using it together—at least they're talking while Tom urinates (it sounds like a man urinating)—although Joan could be standing in the hall. Then she hears them go upstairs, together, into his room. She's glad she's not up to see that part. She hears them get into bed. She falls asleep listening for them to make love.

The sun doesn't wake Joan up. Tom does. "You better get up," he says. "We get up early here." He is standing by the bed in the pale blue tennis shorts she helped him pick out Thursday night in Herman's. Tom isn't tan, although it's August. From this angle, lying in bed with Tom standing beside her, the hair on his legs looks very unattractive. She gets out of bed and stands beside Tom in her Nike T-shirt.

"What should I wear?" she asks. "Do you get dressed up for breakfast?" When can I take a shower? she thinks to herself. Now, or after breakfast? Do they have a shower? She didn't see one in the bathroom last night.

"Not dressed up," says Tom. He pulls his matching blue-and-white-striped shirt over his head and speaks from inside it. "But dressed."

Joan looks out the window. A woman is dragging a black cat on a leash across the lawn. The cat looks dead.

"That's Deborah," says Tom. They both stand by the window and watch Deborah. "I don't know what that is she's got."

"It's a cat," says Joan.

"It looks like a skunk."

"Is your father here, too?" Joan asks. She puts on her

jean skirt, then pulls off her T-shirt.

"I'm not sure," Tom says. "Let's hope not."

In the kitchen, Mrs. Thorenson is cutting up fruit for a fruit salad. She bought kiwifruit at The Fruit Basket just for this weekend, but she is unsure how to slice them. Should she peel them? The fuzzy skin looks unappetizing and vaguely dangerous. Yet, when she tries to peel them, the soft green flesh mushes up. She has, at Fanny Farmer's suggestion, quartered the strawberries, sliced (diagonally) the bananas, sectioned the grapefruit, and balled the cantaloupe with a teaspoon, but Fanny Farmer doesn't mention kiwifruit. The kiwis are hopeless. She throws them away. Good riddance to them, although at ninety-nine cents each it is a shame.

She watches Deborah tie her cat—what was its name, Gilda?—to the rail of the deck and come inside.

"Do you think it's safe to leave him out there?" Deborah asks.

"Of course," Mrs. Thorenson says. Gilbert climbs onto the canvas director's chair and lies in the sun. "Just make sure he doesn't fall off the deck and hang himself."

"He can't," says Deborah. She opens the refrigerator and looks in it. "He has on a harness, not a collar. Have they come down yet?"

"No," says Mrs. Thorenson. "But they're awake."

"She left her soap in the bathroom," Deborah says. "Clinique."

"So?" says Mrs. Thorenson.

"So, nothing. Just FYI."

The morning goes O.K. Mrs. Thorenson's fruit salad is a big hit, the coffee Deborah laced with cinnamon makes the kitchen smell nice, and Joan begins to relax. There is a shower, a nice one with a Water Pik showerhead and plenty of hot water, and after breakfast Joan takes a long shower and changes into her bathing suit.

They all sit on the deck for a while. Deborah lets Gilbert off the leash, and he sits in some bayberry bushes purring and looking dazed. At ten o'clock Mrs. Thorenson and Deborah drive to the airport to pick up Mr. Thorenson, who missed his flight the night before.

Joan and Tom go down to the beach. It's rocky except for one small area that's surrounded by railroad ties and filled with sand—bought sand, Tom explains, sand replaced every summer and after extremely high tides. They keep sacks of it in the boathouse.

But it's like a little oasis, and Tom and Joan lie on it, on an old bedspread that has a Wizard of Oz motif, only Dorothy doesn't look like Judy Garland, she looks like Heidi. She's blonde and dressed in lederhosen.

The blonde, skipping Dorothys unnerve Joan, but when she closes her eyes and traces the indentation down Tom's warm back again and again—a gesture she usually reserves for after they have made love—she begins to feel better, and by the time Deborah appears on the little beach, with Gilbert back on his leash, she's almost happy. It's not so bad here. It's nice.

"Daddy missed that plane, too," Deborah announces. "Mommy's beginning to get worried."

"Can't she call?" asks Tom. He doesn't open his eyes.

"She did. There's no answer." Deborah drops the leash and wades into the waves. Gilbert crouches on the beach looking terrified.

Joan sits up and watches Deborah in the water. When

she was in college, Deborah was married to a Pakistani exchange student. Tom told Joan this, but also told her it is no longer mentioned. His exact words were "dead and buried."

"Have you been in the water yet?" Deborah calls.

"No," Joan shouts, "but I'm hot."

"Come in," Deborah shouts back. "It's great."

Joan gets up and steps over Gilbert, who flinches. She stands with her feet in the moist sand at the edge of the water, allowing the waves to come to her. She feels dizzy standing up.

Deborah splashes in toward shore, peels off her tank top and throws it on the beach. It lands near Gilbert, who bolts up the path toward the house. Deborah runs back out and dives under a wave. She has nothing on under the tank top.

"I forgot to take my contacts out," Joan says to no one: Deborah is underwater, and Tom doesn't hear her.

Deborah's head, brown shoulders, and white breasts slip out of the water and she flings her hair back from her face. "Come on," she calls to Joan. "It's great!"

"I have to take my contacts out," Joan yells. "I'll be right back."

Deborah makes some facial expression that Joan can't interpret: it could be irritation or sympathy or disgust.

Joan touches Tom's back with one of her wet toes, and says, for the third time in as many minutes, "I forgot to take my contacts out. Can I go up?"

"Sure," says Tom. "Would you bring down the suntan lotion? I think my shoulders are getting burned."

"They are," says Joan. "You better be careful. Turn over."

* * *

Mrs. Thorenson is sitting on the deck under a huge lavender-and-white-striped umbrella, drinking orange juice.

"I'm sorry my husband is ruining your weekend," she says, as Joan comes up the path. Her sunglasses have a pink plastic triangle over the nose, which she has flipped up, so it looks like a tiny horn coming out from between her eyes.

Joan was not aware that Mr. Thorenson was ruining her weekend. "Oh, hardly," she says, while she thinks about what she should say. "I'm having a good time."

"I'm not," says Mrs. Thorenson. "Maybe it would be better if he didn't come. Did Tom tell you he's found religion?"

Tom had mentioned something about Mr. Thorenson's newfound religious zeal, saying it was all because the doctors made him give up bridge, because he was getting "obsessive." But Joan isn't sure what this has to do with him missing all these planes: Is he one of those weirdos who try to sell flowers in airports? Surely he's not that bad.

Joan decides to play it safe and resorts to her now standard line. "I've come up to take my contact lenses out," she says. "I'm going in for a swim."

Mrs. Thorenson takes a sip of her drink. An ice cube falls out of the glass and onto the wooden deck, where it quickly begins melting in the sun. The melting ice cube reminds Joan of the speedup movies she used to see of crocuses blooming, only in reverse.

"I didn't know you wore contacts," Mrs. Thorenson says.

"Yes," Joan says. "For years."

"Come here," says Mrs. Thorenson. "Let me see." She

reaches out her tanned hand and motions Joan over. "Are they hard or soft?"

"Hard," says Joan. She bends down and lets Mrs. Thorenson hold her chin and turn her face sideways. She opens her eyes wide. She's looking at a wooden sign nailed to the side of the house that says WELCOME SHIPMATES.

"So you do," says Mrs. Thorenson. Her hot breath lands on Joan's cheek. There is more than juice in that glass, Joan thinks.

Before Joan returns, Deborah gets out of the water and puts her tank top back on. "Where's Gilbert?"

Tom sits up. "He ran up to the house. I don't think he liked it down here."

"Do you like Gilbert?" asks Deborah. She sits down on the bedspread where Joan had been lying, forming a big wet spot.

"He's all right," says Tom. "I don't know."

"You could at least cheer up a little," says Deborah. She puts on her punk sunglasses. "What's the matter?"

"Nothing," says Tom. "Let me try them on."

Deborah gives him the sunglasses. He tries them on. They do things for him. "They look great," says Deborah. She reaches over and takes them off. "But they look greater on me."

"Do you like Joan?" asks Tom.

"Why?" asks Deborah. "Are you going to marry her?"

"I'm going to ask her," Tom says.

"Seriously?" says Deborah. "You're kidding."

"No," says Tom. "I'm serious. At least about asking her."

"I can't believe it," says Deborah. "I thought you just met her."

"At Christmas," Tom says. "Last Christmas." He lies back down. "It's summer now," he says as if it just dawned on him.

"When are you going to ask her?" says Deborah. "I want to watch."

"I'm not sure," says Tom. "Sometime this weekend. When the moment is right."

"Jesus Christ," says Deborah. "I can't believe you're going to get married."

"But do you like her?"

Before Deborah can answer, Joan stumbles onto the beach. "I can't see anything," she says. "Where's the water?"

After lunch Mrs. Thorenson has Tom hold the ladder while she ties TV dinner trays to the cherry tree. Their clatter and reflection scare the birds away. Mrs. Thorenson went out and bought ten macaroni-and-cheese TV dinners (the cheapest) before she realized she could have used aluminum pie plates. The women's magazine had recommended the TV dinner trays, instead of just throwing them away. Mrs. Thorenson doesn't really like cherries—they have pits—but it bothers her that the birds get them. The sea gulls are always sitting fatly under the tree, their breasts stained red.

Joan is sitting on the ground shucking corn for dinner. Some of the silk is picked up and carried off by the breeze, and it hangs like lighted hair in the air. Joan watches it disappear into the pine trees.

Mrs. Thorenson's head is hidden by leaves and TV dinner trays, but Joan is listening to her talk. "I wish this were a peach tree. Wouldn't it be nice if this were a peach tree? This tree was a gift from a woman I never liked. She stayed here one weekend when we first built the house and she gave us this cherry tree as a house gift. I don't remember how it got planted. I remember it sat in a burlap bag for a long time after she left.

"That was back when Daddy came up on the seaplane with Mr. Thomas Friday nights and landed on Great Snake Pond. Do you remember? We'd go over there after dinner and wait on the dock and you and Deborah would have flashlights—it would just be getting dark. And the plane would appear and get closer and closer and land with a splash and Daddy would get out on the dock in his business suit, holding his briefcase, dropped from the sky. Do you remember?"

"No," says Tom. "I must have repressed it."

"Why would you have repressed it?" Mrs. Thorenson asks. A TV dinner tray falls out of the tree.

"I don't know," says Tom. "Maybe it was painful."

"You were probably just too young," Mrs. Thorenson says. "Maybe Deborah remembers. Deborah must."

Tom looks over to see if Joan is watching, and when he sees she is, he mimes kicking the ladder out from under Mrs. Thorenson. Tom is sulking because his shoulders are sunburned. Tom is a sulker, Joan is realizing. When they changed out of their bathing suits, Tom noticed the red streaks beginning to bloom across his white shoulders. He blamed Joan, accusing her of not applying the sunblock properly. As he stands under the tree, he keeps craning his neck to get a better view of his back.

Joan watches, amused, but there's something about the leafy pattern of shadows moving across Tom's mottled skin that makes him look a little leprous from behind. This thought nauseates her, so she concentrates on the corn. When she first met Tom at her old boyfriend's

Christmas party, she thought he was wonderful. He was very good-looking, and a great, tireless dancer, and after the party he insisted they go out for breakfast. On their way home in the cab, Tom shot the stoplights from red to green, and he hit every one, and as the cab flew down the deserted avenue, Joan began to think she might be falling in love. It was very magical. But the next morning she worried it might have been the wicked punch. And ever since it's followed that pattern: Tom will do something nice—buy her flowers, make love to her especially well, invite her to Maine—something that will intoxicate her, but then a few minutes or hours or days later she'll lose interest in him again. One of the reasons she came to Maine was to get a grip on all this and decide one way or another. She pulls the silk off the last ear of corn. She feels lightheaded, but it's not the wine she is drinking that makes her feel giddy. It's something else. What is it? Joan thinks. Then she realizes. It's because she knows she doesn't love Tom. All these months she has been trying to convince herself otherwise. But now—right now—she knows. As she stuffs the last strands of corn silk into the brown paper bag she feels truly out of love with Tom. Everything will change now, she has a feeling, everything will be all right. She laughs. She can't help it.

"What are you laughing at?" asks Tom.

"Nothing," says Joan. "I'm just happy."

"Are you?" says Tom. He smiles. "So am I."

At dinner, at a restaurant called Oysters & Oxes, Tom asks Joan to marry him. The waiter arrives with a bottle of champagne Tom secretly ordered on a trip to the men's room, and the whole uncorking procedure gives Joan some time to think about how she should say no.

Then the waiter is gone, and she's left with Tom sitting across from her, a glass of champagne raised in front of him, repeating his embarrassing proposal. Joan's champagne glass is still on the table and she can feel the bubbly mist cooling her throat.

Tom's serious face glowing sincerely in the candlelight makes her feel sad and guilty. How could she have let things go this far? This is a predicament she associates with movies—old movies—or with her mother's time.

"Marry?" she says, as if it's a word with many shades of meaning.

"Yes," says Tom. "Don't you think we should?"

"No," says Joan.

Tom puts down his champagne glass. "Oh," he says. He picks it up again and drinks from it.

Joan thinks, This is so wrong. She's sure that all the people she knows who are married decided mutually while watching TV or baking bread or wallpapering their apartments. She and Tom do none of these things. They go to the movies and out to dinner once or twice a week and sleep together on the weekends, but they've never been through anything together or gone on a trip or even had a big fight. It's just not a serious relationship. Why doesn't Tom know this? It's scary to think that he can be in love with her on the basis of so little.

She excuses herself and goes down to the women's room. There is a hand-lettered sign that looks like an invitation taped to the mirror, explaining that, since the women's room is below sea level, please don't flush tampons down the toilet.

When she comes back the mussels have disappeared. She drinks some champagne. "I'm sorry," she says. "You surprised me."

"It's O.K.," says Tom. "We can talk about it later."

She should tell him no, never, but she doesn't. She just smiles. "It was very nice of you," she says. "Thank you."

Tom shrugs. He is playing with the champagne cork, making it roll on the table in little lopsided circles. Joan thinks, If I said yes, he'd keep the cork as a souvenir, and every year on the anniversary of this date, he'd bring it out and show it to me.

When they get back to the house Deborah is standing in the sandy driveway. It is windy and the wind seems to blow even the stars around in the sky. Joan is a little drunk.

"Gilbert got away," Deborah announces, as they get out of the car. "I can't find him."

This domestic tragedy immediately cheers Joan; it's a welcome relief from the silent tension between her and Tom. The wind is waking her up, too.

"Gil-bert!" Joan shouts into the blowing bushes.

"I thought I could hear him meowing," Deborah says, "but I can't tell where it's coming from."

They all listen for a minute, but they don't hear Gilbert. Deborah shines her flashlight into the scrubby pine trees. Joan sits on the hood of the car and takes her shoes off. The tops of her feet are sunburnt. "Maybe he's down by the water," she says.

"Maybe he's dead," Tom says.

"I'm going to go look on the beach," Joan says, partly because she wants to see the water at night, partly because she wants to get away by herself. She gives Tom a look she hopes discourages him from joining her.

"Do you want a flashlight?" asks Deborah. "There's another one in the drawer beneath the breadbox."

"No," says Joan. She hops off the car. "It's bright out." She's right: the moon and the stars seem to be unusually —and unnervingly—near, as if they've dropped out of their niches and are falling.

"I'm going to go look over by Cooke's," says Deborah. "There was a dead rabbit over there last weekend Gilbert might have smelled. Come with me," she says to Tom. "I'm scared."

She and Tom walk down the driveway, across the dirt road, and into the woods. Deborah shines the flashlight at the ground; toadstools poke through the matted pine needles, forming little tents.

"So?" says Deborah.

"So, what?"

"So did you ask her?"

"Yes," says Tom. He kicks a toadstool and watches the white floweret fly through the air out of their circle of light. "She said no."

"Oh," says Deborah.

Tom stops walking and leans against a pine tree. He picks some lichen off the bark.

Deborah shines the flashlight at his face. "Are you sad?" she asks.

Tom looks at her, but can't see, because of the bright light in his eyes. "A little," he says. "I don't know."

"I wouldn't be too sad," says Deborah. "She seems like kind of a pill to me."

"Oh," says Tom.

"I mean, I'm sure she's nice. Are you really O.K.?"

"I'm O.K.," says Tom. "I just feel like a fool."

Deborah turns her flashlight off. "Gilbert's not really lost," she says. "I just made that up so I could get you away."

"Did Daddy come?"

"No," says Deborah. "But he called. From Dallas. He said there are a lot of heathens in Dallas."

"There are heathens everywhere," says Tom. "I'm a heathen."

"Don't tell Daddy that," Deborah says. She laughs.

"Where is Gilbert?"

"In my room."

"Maybe Joan will get lost looking for him," says Tom. "Maybe she'll never come back."

"Maybe," says Deborah.

Joan walks around the house and onto the croquet lawn. The wickets grow out of the ground like strange curving reeds. Everything looks different, Joan thinks, when you're drunk and it's dark and windy and your life is changing. All she wants to do is get back to the city and start over again. She's already forgotten about Gilbert.

As she walks down the sloping field of wickets, something catches her eye on the other side of the house—the cherry tree. It's blowing in the wind and looks as if it's trying to shake the TV dinner trays off its limbs, and as Joan watches, one does come off, and sails, gleaming, into the night.

My girlfriend, Ann, is a haircutter. As she cut my hair, I fell in love with her. Every time she held the hand mirror behind my head, I said, "Shorter." Finally, when my scalp threatened to rise through my hair like an expanding eggshell, Ann said she thought she should stop, and I asked her to come have coffee with me. She came, but instead she had iced Red Zinger tea, which stained the skin above her lips pale pink.

I am reminded of her profession today. She is sitting on the ground next to me French-braiding the hair of a Barbie doll. We are running a yard sale for my grandmother, who is moving out of her house, in Connecticut, and into my parents', in California. Because she refuses to fly, Ann and I are driving her cross-country. She likes ships, and wanted to sail.

As my grandmother collected her belongings for this trip, she threw the things she didn't want out the front door and windows of her house. A porcelain lamp shattered on the front walk; I picked up the larger pieces (they gleamed and curved like shells) and swept the tiny shards into the hedge. Ann found the Barbie doll in the rhododendron bush, its slender plastic legs raised like a mutant blossom. We have assembled along the sidewalk what my grandmother discarded. There are stacks of books, and I have just finished arranging the silverware in a row of place settings that stretches from one end of the lawn to the other, as if awaiting picnickers.

The Barbie doll Ann is working on has explosive, waist-length white hair. If she were to become real and walk down the street, heads would turn.

"Does that toaster work?" asks a woman holding a grocery bag. She points at the toaster with her foot. She is wearing espadrilles.

Before I can answer, Ann says, "Yes."

"How much do you want for it?" the woman asks.

"Five dollars," Ann says.

"I might give you three."

"It's a very good toaster," Ann says. "It never burns anything."

"Do you have any brandy snifters?"

"No," says Ann. "But we have a goldfish bowl. I'll give you that and the toaster for five dollars."

"Let me see it."

Ann picks a round vase painted with tulips from a box I have cleverly marked "Etcetera—50¢."

"That's not a goldfish bowl," the woman says.

"So," says Ann. "You wanted brandy snifters." She looks at the vase. "It's pretty. Five dollars for this and the toaster."

"You're sure it works?"

"I'm sure," Ann says. "You should have seen my English muffins this morning. Golden brown." For breakfast Ann ate a soft-boiled egg from an egg cup she found in the kitchen and decided to keep for herself.

"All right," the woman says. Ann puts the vase and the toaster into a shopping bag. The woman gives her some singles and some change. "I hope you don't mind pennies," she says.

Business has been slow all afternoon. Ann is sleeping on the grass, wrapped in a shawl my sister crocheted for my grandmother in Home Ec. Ann was modeling it before she fell asleep in it. The phone rings—seven times, before I realize my grandmother is not going to answer it—and I run inside. When I get to the kitchen the phone has stopped ringing. I can see my grandmother sitting in the backyard.

I go upstairs to smoke a cigarette. Since I officially quit smoking a year ago, I have to smoke in private. It is getting to be a bad habit: in the way I once craved nicotine, I now crave being alone.

I sit on the bed in the front room (we're selling the house "partially furnished") and smoke a Camel Light with dispatch. Ann's suitcase is open on the floor, and there is a bag of gorp on the night table. I eat a few sunflower seeds. They taste as bad as I had anticipated. The only time this stuff tastes good is when you're high.

Last night, after I got into bed in the next room, someone knocked on my door. "Ann?" I whispered.

"No, David," my grandmother said. "It's me." I was surprised, as she had gone to bed much earlier. "Can I come in?" she asked.

She opened the door and looked around the room as if she weren't familiar with it, as if she thought I might have redecorated it or something. She was wearing a matching nightgown-bathrobe-slipper set. Everyone gives her one for Christmas. She has a different set for every night of the year, practically.

"I was just going through some things," she said, "and I wanted to give this to you." She handed me a photograph of a little boy sitting on a dock, his thin legs disappearing into the water. "It's you," she said. "When you were little."

I looked at the picture. The boy was trying to smile, but the sun was in his eyes. His expression was sweetly pained. It was not me. It was my uncle—my mother's brother, my grandmother's son.

"This isn't me," I said. "This is Uncle Ray."

My grandmother took the picture back and looked at it. "This isn't you? It looks like you."

"I'm sure," I said, "I never had a bathing suit like that."

"It does look like Ray, too," she said.

"It is Uncle Ray," I said.

"Well," she said. "You can have it anyway, if you'd like it. It looks like you. I thought it was you."

She gave me the picture and I placed it on my pillow. "Thanks," I said.

"Good night," she said. "Sleep tight." She closed the door but forgot to turn out the light. I got up and turned it off, and when I got back in bed I could feel the photograph against my cheek. It felt as smooth and warm as skin.

Now I put my cigarette out on the heel of my boot, and hide the stub in an empty dresser drawer. Through the window I can see Ann sleeping on the lawn. A middle-aged couple walk along the sidewalk. The man picks a broken camera out of the 50¢ box and pretends to take a picture of Ann. In most pictures, Ann looks stiff and unhappy. She wanted to be a model but was told she did not photograph well, so she switched from modeling school to beauty school. It is too bad the camera is broken, because this picture of Ann sleeping on the front lawn would be beautiful.

Ann wakes up with leaves in her hair, and suggests we get the show on the road. While she throws the unsellable items into the trunk of the car, I search for my grandmother. I find her sitting on the back patio. She has a blanket wrapped around her, and is holding a mug. She looks like someone on the deck of a ship. The wind in the mulberry tree sounds a little like the sea.

"Well," she says. "Have you sold everything? Did you make me pots of money?"

"Not much," I say, answering both questions at once.

"It was all junk," my grandmother says.

"What are you drinking?"

My grandmother looks into the mug but doesn't answer.

"What is it?" I ask again. She shakes her head and hands me the mug. I taste the pale brown liquid. "Is it cider?"

"I forget," my grandmother says. "If it were poison, I'd be dead now."

"So would I," I say. "Ann and I are taking the rest of the stuff to the dump. Then we should leave."

"Who's Ann?" asks my grandmother.

"My girlfriend," I say. I pour the cider on the ground.

"That was your girlfriend? Are you going to get married?"

"No," I say.

"Never?"

"I doubt it," I say.

* * *

At the dump, I sit in the car and listen to the radio while Ann throws the board games and broken appliances over the cliff. We dropped the clothes into a Salvation Army bin outside the A & P. Once, when I was young, I came to the dump at night with my grandmother. There were so many rats it looked to me as if the whole ground were moving. I had my pajamas on and stayed in the car. My grandmother seemed to wade through the rats and tower in the glare from the headlights, tossing her garbage into the darkness.

Ann gets back in the car and wipes her hands on my pants. It is a familial, rather than erotic, gesture.

"My grandmother wants to know if we're getting married," I say. Instead of putting the car in reverse, I turn the engine off.

"What did you tell her?" Ann asks.

"I said yes," I lie.

"Oh," says Ann.

"I said probably in June."

"She asked when?"

"No. I told her. I made that part up."

"What about the part about us getting married?"

"That could be true," I say. "Couldn't it?"

"It could," says Ann. "But it's not. Listen," she continues, as if I were not listening. "I've changed my mind."

"About what?"

"About this," she says, indicating with her dirty hand the car, and beyond it the dump.

"You want something back? I'll climb down and get it. I've done it before."

"No," says Ann. "I mean about going with you to California."

"Oh," I say.

"I'm not going to come," she says. "I can't."

"You can't?"

"I don't want to," she says.

"Why?" I ask. "Why not?"

"There is no good reason, really. I just can't think of a good reason to go. It's so far away. It's going to take so long."

"I thought that was the idea," I say. "To go someplace together."

Ann smiles, and shakes her head. "I called my brother. I've decided. I want you to drop me off in Stroudsburg. It's on Route 80, so it's on your way." She looks at me. "I just can't see myself doing it," she says. "I don't have the energy."

I can see Ann doing it. Ever since she said she would come, I have pictured her doing this: finding good radio stations while I drive through the night, eating scrambled eggs at HoJo's in the morning, practicing swan dives in the indoor pools of hotels. I can picture it all, but I let this pass. I look in the rearview mirror, as if we were being tailed. In it I can see the dump man's little shed. It is surrounded by plastic flowers and flying wooden birds and petrified Bambi-like deer, all rescued—lovingly, I like to think—from the dump.

For a second I think Ann is reaching out to touch my leg. Instead, she turns the ignition key.

Back at the house, we load my grandmother's suitcases for the journey. She insists on sitting in the back seat. She wants the "young people" to sit in front. She says "young people" as if there were a group of us drinking and dancing and throwing Frisbees.

She has lived in this house since 1953, but she doesn't

look back at it as we drive away. She is too busy putting on her seat belt. It is pushed into the crevice behind the back seat, along with the gum wrappers, pennies, and combs. But she digs it out and fastens it. It hangs at her waist, untightened. It is just getting dark, but she could see the house if she looked.

No one says anything for a long time. My grandmother periodically flips the tiny tin lid of the ashtray open and closed. When my mother called me up and told me they were selling my grandmother's house and moving her out to the West Coast, she referred to it as "the big move." "David," she said into the phone, "it's time for the big move." Their phone is on the patio, and I thought I could hear the ocean.

"Is that the ocean?" I asked.

"No," my mother said. "It's your father. He's vacuuming." She told me later, in a letter she sent with all my instructions (". . . use the Visa card for hotels. Get two rooms, but make sure they're adjoining. I leave it up to you whether or not to leave the door open between. . . ."), that my grandmother wasn't putting up any resistance. "Secretly," my mother wrote, "she wants this move more than anyone, I think."

Usually, I think it is smart never to say anything you have rehearsed saying. I have anticipated this silence all day, and all day I've thought about what I could say to transcend it. But now I realize it is an impossible moment, and there is nothing I can say to make us warm to each other. Ann is preoccupied with leaving me, and is no longer interested in my grandmother's big move. She will get out of the car in Stroudsburg, Pennsylvania, and probably forget all about us. She will not wake up tomorrow morning and picture us driving through Ohio. And my grandmother may be cooperating, but she isn't participating. She isn't even looking out the window. In the rearview mirror, I can see her face lowered, her eyes focused on the floor.

We are forty minutes ahead of schedule when we get to the rest stop on Route 80 where Ann has arranged to meet her brother. My grandmother is asleep, her head fallen back against the top of her seat.

"I'm hungry," Ann whispers. "Do you want to get something to eat?"

"O.K.," I say.

"Will she be all right? What if she wakes up?"

"We can leave her a note," I say. "Telling her we're inside."

Ann opens the door and gets out of the car. She does some calisthenics in the parking lot. "Do you have a pen?" I ask Ann.

"I have one," my grandmother says. She doesn't open her eyes.

"What?" I say.

"There's a pen in my bag," my grandmother says. "If you want to leave me a note. There's a little pad, too."

"I guess you're awake," I say.

My grandmother doesn't embarrass me by answering. She continues to feign sleep. "Where are we?" she says. "Are we in California yet?"

"We're in Pennsylvania," I say. "We're waiting for Ann's brother. Do you want to come in?"

"No," my grandmother says. "I'll stay here."

"Can I bring you something?"

"Yes."

"What?"

"A surprise," my grandmother says.

* * *

I sit at a cafeteria table with a cup of black coffee, a glass of seltzer, and a piece of apple pie. The apple pie came with a slice of American cheese. The cheese unnerves me. Ann is in the ladies' room.

I've known Ann for almost a year. When we started seeing each other, she asked me to electrocute her facial hairs. She had quite a bit of bleached blond hair above her lip and on her chin. Every night before we went to bed, she got out this little gadget that looked like an electric toothbrush, and I touched the needlelike wand to the follicles of exactly ten hairs. They would pop, then shrivel up, and never come back. Ann believed it was dangerous to zap more than ten hairs a night. I was included in this ritual for practical reasons; Ann said that performing electrolysis on yourself was not recommended. It all had to do with being safely grounded.

Now Ann's face is hairless and not at all unsightly. I will spend six weeks in California and when I come back to New York I will not look Ann up. I really will not.

There is a guy about my age sitting at another table. He raises his coffee cup and smiles at me. I finish my pie (leaving the cheese) and walk over to his table.

"Are you Teddy?" I ask.

"What?"

"Are you Ann's brother? Teddy?"

"No," he says. "I'm Julie's brother. Rob."

"Oh," I say. "I thought you were someone else."

"Maybe that's Freddy," he says. He points to a man buying cigarettes.

"Teddy," I correct. "He's too old."

"I feel like I should try to sell you some pot or pick you up or something," the guy says. "But I don't do either of those things."

"Oh," I say.

"You can sit down," he says. "If you want."

"I'm waiting for my girlfriend," I say. "She's in the bathroom."

"I thought you were waiting for Freddy."

"Him, too," I say. I sit down and look at the sugar packets. They have pictures of historical sights on them. I don't recognize any. Some of them seem to be made up. Ann comes out of the bathroom but sits at the table with my coffee and her seltzer. She picks up the slice of cheese as if it were a fish.

"That's my girlfriend," I say.

"Now all you need is Teddy," he says. He is eating French fries from a red-checkered cardboard boat. They are covered with ketchup and salt. They look wonderful. If I knew him just a little better I would ask for one.

When I sit down at the other table, Ann says, "You know, you don't have to wait. Teddy'll come."

"I'll wait," I say. "I don't mind. What if he doesn't come?"

"He'll come," Ann says.

I think for a moment but realize there is nothing left for me to say. So I say, "O.K."

Ann watches the bubbles in her glass. "I feel terrible about this," she says. "I know I said I'd come with you, but I just can't."

"I understand," I say.

Ann looks at me to see if I understand, sees I do not, and lowers her eyes. "I just can't," she repeats. "It wouldn't be fair."

I go up to the counter and get a large order of French fries and two tiny envelopes of ketchup.

When I get back to the car, my grandmother is gone. I

put the fries on the hood and sit beside them. Just when I'm about to swallow my pride and go back inside and ask Ann to look for her in the bathroom, I see my grandmother in the back parking lot, walking between two trailer trucks. Every few steps, she pauses and bends over, as if she had lost something under them, or were checking the pressure in their tires.

I run across a small, wet lawn and stand on the curb. "Grandma," I call. A man in a white apron is smoking on the kitchen steps. I hear him laugh.

"What?" my grandmother says. She walks from one pool of light into another.

"What are you doing?" I say. "You scared me."

She doesn't answer.

"You could have got hit," I say. "Or fallen down."

"I could have," she says. "I didn't."

"I was worried," I say. "Let's go."

"What's the rush?" my grandmother says.

"I don't know," I say. "It's cold. I got you French fries. They're getting cold."

Even though there are no cars back here, my grandmother looks both ways before she crosses the service road. I take her arm and escort her across the grass. She takes high, halting steps, like a cat. I open the car door, and close it, carefully, behind her. I get in my side of the car. The French fries are still on the hood. I climb back out and retrieve them. They are still warm but the ketchup is gone. Some creep stole it. I get back in the car and hand the fries to my grandmother. She holds them in her cupped hands the way she once held injured birds, softly but tightly, so they don't fly away.

The Last Possible Moment

I'm sitting in my kitchen watching my roommate Ross. He's standing at the sink, trying to find the hole in his bicycle's inner tube so he can patch it. He lowers it section by section into the filled basin, waiting for the tiny trail of bubbles to rise. Ross isn't really my roommate. He moved in because his mother has come to visit, and she doesn't know he is living with his girlfriend, Laura. She thinks he's still engaged to this girl he saw in college, who's now in veterinary school. We're pretending to be roommates.

Mrs. Ross is displeased with Ross. She's come up to Portland from Boston to try to get him to move back and get a "real" job. She's arranged an opening as a physical therapy aid in the hospital where she works. All through dinner—Ross had made scallops and vegetables in the wok—she talked about the joys of splints and hot packs and acupressure. Now she's watching TV in the living room. She's giving up on Ross.

Ross is a bartender, and if he doesn't get his tire patched he'll be late for work. I'd drive him, but my car broke down last night in front of my ex-girlfriend's house. I don't have the money to fix it, let alone tow it.

I wipe the crumbs off the kitchen table into my hand with a damp sponge. Usually I wash them down the drain but since the sink is full of water and inner tube I hold them in my hand. They're mostly little bits of celery.

"What are you doing tonight?" Ross asks.

"Nothing," I say. I stand beside him at the sink and watch the inner tube. It's coiled like a black snake. "I don't have any money. I don't get my check till Tuesday. All I have are food stamps."

"You could go grocery shopping," Ross suggests.

"I have all day to go grocery shopping. I'd kind of like to do something more exciting with my evenings."

"Come down to the Angel. It's local-talent night. That's always good for a laugh. Bring Doreen." Doreen is Mrs. Ross.

"What?" Mrs. Ross shouts from the living room.

"Nothing," says Ross. Bubbles rise from a pinprick in the black skin. "There," Ross whispers. "Got you."

"Another thing, Quentin." Mrs. Ross stands in the kitchen door. "You could live in Aunt Judy's apartment. She'll be in Central America for six months."

Ross left for work—on his patched bicycle—so I'm walking Mrs. Ross back to her hotel, up my deserted street. Mrs. Ross's high heels click along the sidewalk. I walk on the grass verge along the street, barefoot, carrying a sneaker in each hand. Each year I try to stay barefoot until the last possible moment.

"I don't understand Quentin," Mrs. Ross says. "When he told us he was moving to Portland neither his father nor I objected—of course he's past the age where we could have objected had we wanted to—but things seem to have gotten out of hand. I don't like to think he's settling down up here. What's this bar like where he works?"

"It's a nice bar," I say. "They have live entertainment, sometimes. He makes pretty good money."

"That's not the point," Mrs. Ross says. "I mean, we're glad he has a job. . . ." She doesn't finish her sentence because she knows I don't have a job anymore. I worked during the summer as the "first mate" on one of those boats that take tourists around the bay and the islands. I got laid off the week after Labor Day, when Captain Andy sailed the boat down to Florida for the winter. I could have gone with him, but at that point I was still seeing Polly, and I thought it would be easy to find another job.

We're walking up Polly's street. I've purposely steered us this way in the hope that I might see her. During the summer, after dinner, we always hung out in her front yard. I would work on my car—it was running pretty good there, for a while—and Polly would practice her baton twirling. We were both on a self-improvement kick: we had picked things we wanted to do but couldn't, and all summer we tried to learn them. We bought books and everything.

Polly's house is dark. Jasper, her cat, is sitting on the front steps. He doesn't like me. We pass my dead car parked at the curb. It feels weird to see it there, and not acknowledge it in some way.

"This is my car," I say. I touch the hood, which is still a little warm from the sun. Mrs. Ross looks at it. I don't think she believes me.

We walk up the hill to Congress Street in silence, and

then past the lighted windows of the clothes stores. The mannequins stare at us through the yellow cellophane that shields them from the sun. Outside the hotel, under the movie theater–like marquee, Mrs. Ross touches me on my bare forearm, and says, "Do you want to come up for a second? I have a proposition to make."

When I leave the hotel I walk down toward the seaport to visit Laura. She works in Cone Heads, an ice-cream store. When I go in she's sitting behind the glassed-in tubs of ice cream, reading. Laura was my friend before she started seeing Ross. Laura and I went to college together and rented a house downtown with some other people our last two years. We'd stay up late at night and play Risk and talk. Those were good days.

"Hi," she says. "I was hoping you'd come by." She puts her book face down on the counter. It's *The Green Hat.* I sit down at one of the little metal tables. "Did Ross fix his tire?"

"Yes," I say. "I just walked Mrs. Ross home. My fun for the evening."

"The evening is just beginning," Laura says. "Do you want some ice cream?"

I look at the ice cream. It all looks purple or green. "I don't think so."

"I'll make you something special," Laura says. "I'll create." She raises the lid of the case and begins scooping ice cream into a submarine-shaped plastic boat. Laura is trying to get a job as a chef. Portland is supposed to be a very high-quality city in the restaurant department. Laura has this book that rates the cities, and Portland is in the top ten. That's why she moved to Portland. I came to visit her the weekend after graduation and just stayed. I was supposed to be in New York auditioning for acting agents but I was scared. Portland seemed like a safe place.

"Mrs. Ross offered me the job," I say. "She's given up on Ross."

"At the hospital?" Laura asks. She wipes her forehead with the back of her hand and then continues scooping.

"Yeah," I say. "It pays fourteen thousand dollars and has three weeks vacation and I get to join a union."

"I thought you hated unions," Laura says.

"I hate all membership organizations," I say. "But I've never been in a union."

"I can't picture you in a union," Laura says. "What kind of job is it?"

"I'd give patients whirlpool baths, put hot packs on their legs and stuff. They would teach me how to give massages and electro-shock therapy."

"It sounds gruesome," says Laura. "You're not thinking of taking it?" She comes around from behind the counter and puts her creation on the little table. Then she sits down across from me. I don't say anything, because I realize I am thinking about taking it.

"I can't picture you giving people baths," Laura says.

"Whirlpools," I correct. I taste the ice cream. "Is this licorice?"

"Sambuca," says Laura. "Is it good?"

"It's too weird to be good," I say. I hand her the plastic spoon and she tastes it.

"It's different," she says. "No one's buying it. I think because they can't pronounce it. If they just called it licorice it would sell."

"I doubt it."

"Don't go to Boston," Laura says. "It's a horrible town."

"I know. But I'm running out of money. I can't pay my rent on unemployment. Plus I'm going crazy. I need a job."

"There might be an opening here," Laura says. "If Anthony gets into law school."

"It's not what I had in mind," I say.

"It's better than nothing," Laura says. "We'd have fun working together. You might as well get paid for all the time you spend in here. Polly came in before."

"We broke up," I say.

"I know you broke up. Does that mean I can't mention her ever again?"

I shrug.

"Do you want me to tell you a secret?" asks Laura.

"I don't know. Does it concern Polly?"

"No," says Laura. "It concerns me."

"O.K., then."

"Since Ross moved in with you—this sounds terrible, I know—but since he's moved out I've been pretty happy. I like having the place to myself. He gets on my nerves, I think."

"Ross?"

"Yes, Ross."

"What does that mean?" I ask. "Why did you tell me that?" I'm playing with my gray ice cream, forming culverts down the side of a granite mountain. Laura watches me.

"I don't know," she says. "It's just a secret. Did Polly get on your nerves?"

"I didn't live with Polly."

"You kind of lived with Polly," Laura says.

"I don't want to talk about it," I say.

"Do you want to go get a drink? God knows, no one's going to care if I close a little early."

"I don't have any money," I say. "All I have are food stamps, and you can't buy alcohol with them. I've tried."

"If you help me close up, I'll buy you a drink." We get up, and as I lift the tubs of ice cream out of the display case and carry them back into the walk-in freezer, Laura stacks the wrought-iron chairs on top of the tables: one overturned on the lap of the other. When I'm done lugging the ice cream, I stand by the door and Laura counts the cash, her lips moving silently. Moths paste themselves against the screen, and when I rub my sticky fingers against the mesh behind them, they don't fly away. They bat their chalky wings and cling tighter.

I met Polly in Cone Heads. Now she works as a cameraperson at Station 2, filming the news and local talk shows, but last summer she worked here. Laura got her job when she quit. I first kissed Polly in the walk-in freezer last July: our chests pressed warmly together, chilled air surrounding us. Polly rubbed my bare, goose-pimpled arms with her hands. It was an odd sensation, kissing in the freezer: it made me feel especially in love.

The Angel is right across the street from the pier where *The Urchin,* Captain Andy's boat, used to dock. I got the job on the boat because Andy was impressed with my voice. I majored in acting in college, and Andy thought he was really smart to hire a trained actor to do the narration. Of course the boat is gone, but the sign is still hanging outside the little hut where Andy's wife sold tickets. It says, "Cool off! See the Rocky Coast of Maine! Watch the Seals! Feed the Seagulls! $3!" I never saw a seal all summer, except for a dead one that washed up on Crescent Beach. Seal Rock was the high point of every trip, though. When we got there we'd turn off the motor—so as not to scare the seals—and drift. Everyone would crowd to one side of the deck, and I'd whisper into the microphone to stay still and watch the water. It was embarrassing for everyone involved. If it was the morning, I'd claim the seals usually appeared in the afternoon, and vice versa. After a few minutes we'd turn the motor back on and take off. Fortunately the sea gulls always wanted to eat, and that cheered people up. I'd hand everyone a slice of white bread. Some people would ignore the sea gulls and eat it themselves. They thought it was a snack.

In the Angel, Laura and I split a pitcher of beer and listen to some local talent: a woman singing "You Light Up My Life," and a man doing performance art with a clock radio and a dog. Polly and I used to come to the Angel when she finished filming the news. We'd discuss current events and drink Sea Breezes. In the summer you could sit on the roof. The stars always seemed unusually close, and the more Sea Breezes you drank the closer they seemed to get. When we left we'd run across to the pier and kiss in the wind.

Laura and I leave the Angel about 1:30. There's something about coming out of a noisy bar late at night that makes things seem especially quiet. We walk up the cobblestone street, past a gallery where the paintings are hung in the windows on chains.

At the top of the street there is a little park with picnic tables and Laura sits down at one. I lean against the fence.

"You know what I said before? About Ross?" Laura asks.

"Yeah," I say.

"I shouldn't have said that. I didn't mean it like it sounded. I just meant that it's different living by yourself, and kind of nice. . . . I don't know. I didn't mean that I don't want Rossie to move back in. Did you think I did?"

"No," I lie.

"Good," says Laura. "Do you want to come over for some tea?"

"I have to move my car," I say. "It's illegally parked on the wrong side of the street."

"I thought it was broken."

"It is," I say. "I'll push it."

"Do you need help?"

"No," I say. I walk Laura partway home, and then walk over to Polly's. The car is at Polly's because she has a driveway she let me park in, and when we broke up I tried to move my car but I only got as far as the street. It was as if the car refused to leave Polly, even if I did. I get in the car and put it in neutral. Polly has left a book I lent her—*Portrait of the Artist as a Young Dog*—on the driver's seat. I open it up to see if there's a note. There isn't. Polly and I broke up because I wouldn't "open up enough" to her. She said she got to know me up to a point but as things continued I didn't "reveal myself" anymore, and she felt she was wasting her time. She told me this in the tech booth at the TV studio, a tiny, soundproof room. Then she filmed the eleven-o'clock news. I went home and watched it in bed, picturing Polly's hands guiding the camera. I hoped it might shake, so I'd know she was upset, but it didn't.

I get out and push the car, reaching through the open window to steer it at the same time. Polly comes out of her house and stands on the front lawn, watching me.

She's barefoot and wearing a bathrobe. My car gently hits the one in front of it and I swear.

"Do you want some help?" Polly says. "I could steer." She walks across the lawn, gets in the passenger door and slides across the front seat. "O.K.," she says.

I walk around to the back of the car and start pushing. It glides out into the street and Polly steers it toward the opposite curb. She has both hands on the wheel. When it is safely and legally parked, Polly sticks her head out the window. "Get in," she says. I get in the passenger side and pick up the book. "I wanted to give that back," Polly says. "I hate people who keep books that are lent to them."

"Why did you come out here?" I ask.

"Because you needed help," she says.

"This is hopeless," I say. "I can't stand seeing you."

Polly sighs and rests her chin on the steering wheel. "Portland's a small town," she says. "We can't not see each other."

Polly looks over at me and smiles, then closes her eyes. She's braided her hair but left the end unfastened and it's gradually unraveling. I feel like if we sit here long enough it will all come loose. The first night Polly and I slept together I told her I was inarticulate. She laughed, disbelievingly, against my throat. Then she began asking me a series of very specific, yet irrelevant, questions: Did I like artichokes? Had I ever been in a car accident? Did I floss my teeth? Could I water ski? As I answered, she asked more questions, stroking my hair, spinning me into a web of false intimacy. Polly knew I ate an apple, core and all, that sometimes I didn't wear underwear, that I wanted not to be an actor but a rock star, but in the end this wasn't enough for her. She wanted to know what I was thinking, what I felt about things.

The next morning we woke up and went out for breakfast together, then shopping, then to the art museum.
Then we sat outside on a bench in the sun. Polly asked
me if I wanted to go to the movies, and I realized for the
first time what it meant to be in love: It means you sleep
with someone, eat granola and blueberries with them, buy
sneakers with them, kiss them in the Winslow Homer
room, and then go see *Lili Marleen.* I realized I wasn't in
love. It was too much. I felt like I had been with Polly
forever, and had to get away for a while. Or, rather, I felt
like I had been away from myself for too long. So I said
no, and we made plans to see each other the next week
and I ran home feeling relieved and happy but I called her
the next night because by then I was lonely again.

Polly opens her eyes. She is still smiling.

"Remember those questions you used to ask me?" I say.
"Maybe they were the wrong ones."

"I shouldn't have had to ask you all those questions in
the first place," Polly says.

"But maybe they were just the wrong ones. Ask me
some more."

"What are you going to do about your car?" she asks.

"Ask me a real question."

"What are you thinking?"

I think for a moment before I answer. I want to say the
right thing. "You know my dream?" I say, although it's
not really a dream. It's more a feeling I get, as if a moment
from my future has found its way back to me. It inhabits
me for a few seconds—before I fall asleep, when I'm driving late at night—at odd times. I feel myself kneeling on
a lawn, adjusting a sprinkler. It's early summer, and the
grass is soft and green, and without looking I know I'm
outside a house, and I also know that inside the house

there's a woman who's my wife—she's probably putting our children to bed, pulling down the shades in their room, watching me kneel beside the cool spray of water. It's this perfect moment.

"You mean the sprinkler thing?"

"Yeah," I say.

"What about it?" Polly asks. "You know what I think about that dream." Polly thinks my dream is retrograde. "Fifties" is the word she used.

"Can you see me doing that?"

"Adjusting a sprinkler?"

"No," I say. "Being married. Owning a house. Having children. Coming home from work and watering the lawn."

"I don't know," Polly says. "I suppose."

"I can't," I say.

"Well, there's no use worrying about it," Polly says.

"Of course there is," I say. "It's what I want. Sometimes I think I was brought up all wrong. I was brought up too happily."

"That's absurd," Polly says.

"No," I say. "It's not. Everything I want is obsolete. You're right: it is retrograde. I mean, who comes home and waters their lawn anymore. Who has a lawn? Who comes home?"

"Plenty of people." Polly motions out the window at the dark lawns. "See."

"These aren't real lawns," I say. "They're rented."

Polly gets out of the car and stands in the street. She waits a moment, then closes the door.

"I'm thinking of moving to Boston," I say. "Ross's mother can get me a job in a hospital."

"Do you want to move to Boston?"

"No," I say. "I want to stay here. I want to come inside with you. I want to go down to the Angel and have a Sea Breeze."

"I think maybe you should move to Boston," Polly says. "I think it might work out well for you." She walks around to my side of the car and stands on the grass.

"You're going inside?"

"Yes," says Polly.

"Wait," I say. "Let's do something. I don't have any money, but we can go for a ride. Come for a drive."

"Your car is broken," Polly says. I can tell she is trying to be patient and nice.

"Maybe it will start now," I say. "If it starts will you come for a ride?" I slide over to the driver's seat.

"No," says Polly. "I'm going to bed. I'm tired. Good night. I'm sorry if I shouldn't have come out but I didn't want you to wreck your car."

"It already is wrecked," I say.

Polly looks down at her bare feet for a few seconds, then turns around and goes inside. I sit in the car, hoping she will come back out, or open her window and call for me to come up. But she does neither; I see her bedroom light turn on and then quickly off and I know she's in bed.

I've always thought that I'd wait out the winter in Portland and join up with Captain Andy again next summer, but suddenly there doesn't seem much point in hanging around. Maybe Portland isn't such a great place to be in winter. It's fun in the summer, with Sea Breezes and ice-cream cones and Polly standing on the front lawn, throwing her baton up into the evening, where it twirls and disappears for a second into the darkening sky, as if God has caught it, then reappears and falls, still twirling, into Polly's waiting fingers.

I can remember lying on my bare back underneath my car, watching Polly's ankles box-step as she practiced her twirling, and I didn't feel so great, and I don't know why, because those were good days. I should have been euphoric.

I'm not surprised when my car starts, only a little afraid. I rev the engine, testing it, and myself. Before it can die, I pull out into the street and take off. By the time Polly jumps out of her bed and rushes outside, I'll be turning the corner.

In order to enter the MBA program at Columbia in the fall, I had to take calculus in the summer. I was offered two options: an eight-week, slow-paced course or a three-week intensive. Although the last math course I took was trigonometry my junior year in high school, I chose the three-week course, on the principle that things you are scared of are things you shouldn't dwell on too long. I'd finish calculus in July, spend August at the beach, and start school with a tan.

The first Monday of class, the air-conditioning was broken. I had made the mistake of wearing a denim dress, and as the morning progressed, I felt the back of it getting wetter and wetter. The teacher must have known about the air-conditioning because he was wearing khaki shorts and a white T-shirt. He didn't look at all like a teacher—he looked more like a very old Boy Scout or a very young forest ranger. No one knew he was the teacher until he started teaching, which he did hesitantly, almost apologetically. I could tell right away he had never taught before.

The class met from nine to twelve and then from

twelve-thirty to three-thirty. By noon the blackboard was so dusty from erased equations the teacher had to wash it with a sponge and a bucket of water. I went outside and sat on the front steps of the building and ate my tabbouleh-and-pita-bread sandwich. I read over my notes, which already filled about half of the new notebook I'd bought in Lamston's that morning. I couldn't make any sense of them. I'd have to write neater.

The air-conditioner in the hall worked, so I went back up and stood outside the classroom door and drank from a water fountain. I had to lean way down into the curved white basin to reach the weak spurt of water.

When I stood back up the forest ranger was standing beside me holding his bucket of chalky water.

"Will you do me a favor?" he asked.

"What?" I said.

"Will you dump this in the women's room? The men's is locked."

"Sure," I said.

Instead of handing me the bucket, he started walking down the hall. I followed him. Outside the women's room he gave me the bucket and opened the door. He held it open and watched me pour the water down the sink.

He took the bucket back, and we walked down the hall. "You were smart," I said, "to wear shorts."

He looked down at his shorts, as if he had forgotten he was wearing them. He opened the door of the hot classroom and we went in. We were the only ones there. I sat at the desk I had chosen in the morning—in the back row —and he began filling the blackboard with new, harder, equations.

* * *

I was subletting an apartment from a friend of mine, Alyssa. Actually, I wasn't subletting it: her parents owned it, and she had gone to Europe for the summer, so I was staying there, paying the bills, watering the ferns, and feeding the two long-haired, exotic, nasty cats.

It was a huge apartment. The more I saw other people's apartments the more I began to realize how extraordinary this one was: it was full of space. The living room was as big as most apartments, with its two leather couches facing one another across from the fireplace. There was a long hall with a thin Persian runner unraveling along the wooden floor, two bedrooms, an eat-in kitchen, and even a pantry full of glass hutches in which hung dozens of globular wineglasses, like a laboratory.

The evening after the first day of class, I was trying to make cucumber soup without a recipe or a blender when the phone rang. It was an old-fashioned black wall phone in the pantry, where it always seemed to ring louder on account of the glass.

"Hello," I said.

"Is Julie there?" a man asked.

"This is Julie," I said. I never say "This is she." Something about speaking that properly unnerves me.

"Julie? This is Stephen?"

"Stephen?" I repeated. I didn't know any Stephens in New York. I didn't know any men here, actually, except for Ethan, my older sister Debbie's creepy ex-husband, and a cute man named Gerry I met a few nights before in the greengrocer's. I'd helped him pick out a cantaloupe.

"From calculus," the man said.

"Oh," I said. "Which one are you?"

"The teacher," he said. "The one who stands in front."

I laughed, and so did he, then I stopped laughing because I suddenly thought he must be calling to tell me I'd have to drop the class. They must have some system where they weed the hopeless students out immediately. I saw my whole career—business school, New York, executive suites, tailored suits—going down the drain. And so quickly.

"What do you want?" I said rudely.

"I don't know," he said. "To see how I did. I've never taught calculus before."

"Really?" I said. "Never?"

"Well, not for six straight hours."

"Oh," I said.

"So how was I?"

"I've never taken calculus," I said. "Not even an hour. I'm the wrong person to ask."

"Did you understand everything?"

"No," I said.

"Oh. Maybe I should go slower." Then he paused, and said, "Do you want to go out for dinner sometime?"

"Dinner?" I said, as if this was a complicated theorem that needed some explaining.

"Well," he said. "Maybe just a drink."

"No," I said. "Dinner's fine. Dinner's good."

Stephen and I ate dinner the next night in the garden of a restaurant, under a dogwood tree. White blossoms fell into my soup and across the lavender tablecloth when the wind blew. We had met outside the restaurant, and for a minute I didn't recognize him. I had only seen Stephen in his Boy Scout shorts, and that was the only way I could picture him. He didn't look as cute in his green fatigue pants and pink oxford shirt. He could have been anyone.

"So," Stephen said, once our small talk had been run through and our soup delivered. "End my suspense. Why are you taking calculus?"

"I have to," I said. "I'm going to business school."

"I knew it," Stephen said. "Everyone's going to business school. My mother's going to business school."

"Did you teach her calculus?"

"No. I got my math genes from her. My father's mathematically illiterate. He's a painter."

"So am I," I said.

"What, a painter?"

"No," I said. "An illiterate."

"Oh," he said. "Well, you can still learn calculus. It just takes longer."

"Can I learn it by September?"

"Sure. If you get a tutor."

"A tutor?"

"Well, yeah. You're going to have to devote all your time to learning calculus. It's a new way of thinking for people like you. We're talking twelve-hour days, seven days a week."

"Why am I doing this?" I said. "It sounds horrible."

"I don't know," Stephen said. "Why are you doing this?"

I spooned my soup, pushing the blossoms aside.

"I don't know," I finally said. "I felt like my life was going nowhere, like it needed a big change. I've been living in Michigan," I said, as if that explained things.

"Where?"

"Ann Arbor. I went to school there."

"What did you study? I assume it wasn't math."

"French. I can hardly speak it anymore."

"What did you do with a French major?"

"Nothing. I was stenciling wicker furniture. I was making pretty good money, for Ann Arbor, at least, but I got sick of it. There was nowhere to go. So I figured I needed an MBA."

I didn't mention that my boyfriend, Tim, made the wicker furniture and that I had lived with him for five years and been engaged for one of them (the fourth). Most of going to business school had to do with breaking with Timmy.

The waiter came and took our soup away.

"I don't know," I said. "Do you think this is all a big mistake?"

"Fools can get MBA's," Stephen said.

"But they have math genes," I said.

"You have math genes," Stephen said. "They just have to be aroused."

I laughed.

"No, really," he said. "They're there. It's like Pygmalion. I could take you on. I'll transform you into a math whiz."

The leaves of the dogwood tree started shaking above us. I looked up and saw the sky glowing as if the sun had set all over, not in just one spot. I could feel the drops of rain above us, falling: heavy, sooty drops. I stood up and put my bag over my shoulder.

"What's the matter?" said Stephen. He thought I was leaving.

"It's going to rain," I said. "Look."

We were the first couple in the empty restaurant, and we got a table right inside the terrace doors. Watching the rain fall in the deserted garden, I felt wise and intuitive and in touch, if not with calculus, at least with the weather.

* * *

The next night—the third night of class—my official tute-
lage began. Stephen arrived at my door with a calculator
and a bunch of freesias.

"This is some building," he said. "The elevator is about
the size of my apartment."

"It's not mine," I said. "I'm subletting it."

"Oh," Stephen said. "And I thought I had found an
heiress." He handed me the flowers.

"Then you should meet Alyssa." I went into the
kitchen but Stephen walked into the living room, then
down the hall, and into the kitchen through the pantry.
"Do you want something to drink? All I really have is beer
and cranberry juice."

"I'll just have water," Stephen said. He took an overturned glass from the dish drain and filled it from the tap.
I had been nervous about this rendezvous, but there was
something reassuring about watching Stephen's Adam's
apple bob as he gulped the water: he did it as if he'd been
drinking water in my kitchen for years.

Stephen was a better tutor than a teacher. He began by
asking me what I didn't understand. I said just about
everything, so we started at the beginning and as he explained things I asked questions, not letting him continue
until I understood. We moved from the dining-room table
to the living-room couch, and when I finally felt like I
understood the first three days of calculus—about one
o'clock in the morning—I put my calculus book on the
floor and my feet on the couch. We were sitting on opposite ends of the leather couch, facing each other, our legs
entangled between us. He was the kind of person, I noticed, whose second toe is longer than his big toe. My toes
are perfectly proportional, and I set a standard by them.

"You have very long toes," I said. I touched them. "They're kind of ugly."

Stephen yawned and peered down his body at his toes. "It comes with the math genes," he said. "It's part of the package."

When I was growing up, my father was an engineer for NASA, and my mother taught home economics. Now they're both retired and are in business together. They've bought a series of what my father calls "exploitable" houses—barns and shacks and even abandoned churches —which they live in and jointly convert into luxurious summer homes and then resell for no small profit. My father does the outside and my mother the inside, or, as they put it, my father builds the nest and my mother feathers it. They are never in one house for more than a year. My mother gets attached to some of them, but my father insists on selling them. He thinks it's important for people their age to keep moving, as if you'd petrify if you lived in the same house for a few years.

I went up to see them—and the boathouse they were restoring in upstate New York—the first weekend of calculus, although Stephen thought I should stay in New York and study. I told him I'd study at the lake. I intended to: I packed my huge calculus book in my knapsack, and even did a few problems on the plane, but by the time I switched to a six-seater in Syracuse, calculus didn't seem to matter anymore. In the city, with the straight streets and glass walls and constant noise, calculus could be accommodated, but in the tiny plane, gliding over trees and lakes all fading away beneath me into the growing darkness, calculus faded away, too. The numbers and arrows and symbols seemed foolish, so I put my book away and watched the lights come on in the houses below.

Saturday morning I helped my mother upholster a dock that extended around two sides of the house. My parents were converting it into a veranda, covering it with grass-colored indoor-outdoor carpeting. My mother was treading water, outfitted with flippers, mask, snorkel, and staple gun. She looked like Jacques Cousteau. Her job was to swim under the dock and affix the carpeting to the underside; I was supposed to hold it in place and smooth out the wrinkles.

My job was easy. I found the best way to hold the carpet flat and in place was to just lie on the section we were working on. I unhitched my bathing-suit straps and opened my calculus book. I could hear my mother slurping around in the water beneath me, attacking the dock with her staple gun. When she pulled the carpet for a snugger fit, my mechanical pencil rolled off into the weedy water.

In a few minutes my mother swam out from under the dock. She raised the mask so it stuck out from the top of her bathing cap, and crossed her tanned arms on the dock.

"I lost my pencil," I said. "It rolled off."

My mother looked at my calculus book and said, "Can you really do that stuff?"

"Not yet," I said. "It's supposed to click and all make sense at some point."

"The only nice thing about being an old woman is that I was spared new math. I remember when I had to teach metric conversion I was a loony case. Your father had to do a guest lecture on the metric system. We made vichyssoise. All the girls fell in love with him. They had never seen a man cook before. What ever happened to all that?"

"What?"

"The metric system. Don't you remember? We were supposed to convert. They even had commercials on TV about it: 'America Goes Metric.' What happened?"

"I don't know," I said. "I guess they gave up."

"I like inches," my mother said. "I'd miss inches. It's too bad we're not closer to New York. Daddy could help you with your calculus. He used to help Debbie."

"My teacher says it's all genetic," I said. "He thinks my math genes just have to be aroused."

"Aroused?" My mother pushed away from the dock and floated on her back. The skirt of her bathing suit fanned out around her thighs. I looked up into the bright sky and closed my eyes. The first night Stephen and I slept together, he whispered numbers into my ear: long, high numbers—distances between planets, seconds in a life. He spoke as if they were poetry, and they became poetry. Later, when he fell asleep, I leaned over him and watched, trying to picture a mathematician's dreams. I concluded that Stephen must dream in abstract, cool designs like Mondrian paintings.

"Have you heard from Tim?" my mother asked.

"No," I said. I could feel the green turf pressing into my cheek and hear my mother making tiny splashing sounds, listlessly circumventing the lily pads. "We're not calling each other."

"Don't you wonder how he is?"

I opened my eyes. My mother was treading water, moving her arms and legs very gracefully and slowly, making the least possible effort to stay afloat.

"Actually," I said, "I'm seeing someone else."

"Already? Who?"

"You don't know him," I said.

"Well, I assume I don't know him. That's why I'm asking."

"The teacher," I said.

"The calculus teacher? The geneticist?"

"Yes," I said.

"Oh, honey," my mother said. She sounded sad. "Just remember you're on the rebound. Be careful. Especially with a calculus teacher."

"I'm not on the rebound."

"What do you call it, then?" My mother picked a piece of duckweed out of the water, fingered it, then tossed it a few feet away. A small fish rose and mouthed the surface of the water, nipping at it. I thought for a moment. I sat up and put my legs in the water. The fish swam away. I was mad at my mother for bringing up Tim, as I had been doing a pretty good job of forgetting about him.

"It's not a rebound," I said. "It's a new life. It has nothing to do with Ann Arbor or Timmy or wicker."

But my mother wasn't listening. She was looking at the bottom of the lake. "Look," she said. "Your pencil." She did a quick surface dive. I watched her white legs kick down into the dark water. In a moment she popped back up, and tossed my pencil onto the dock.

Stephen and I had, in our one short week together, established a ritual. We went out together after class for a beer. The middle of the afternoon, I discovered, was a nice time to frequent bars. I'd never much liked them at night in Ann Arbor when they were noisy and crowded and dark and sticky. But in the afternoon no one played the juke-box, the sun shone in the open door, and the people in the soap operas swam through their complicated lives on the

TV above the bar like fish in an aquarium.

Stephen was drawing a diagram on a soggy cocktail napkin, trying, as always, to explain something I didn't understand. I was half watching him and half watching a large white cat thread himself through the legs of the bar-stools, savoring the touch of each leg against his fur.

"See," Stephen said, pushing the napkin across the table. I looked at it but couldn't make any sense of it, so I turned it around.

"No," Stephen said. "This way." He turned it back around.

Something about the blurry diagram on the cocktail napkin depressed me. I couldn't believe it had come to be an important part of my life. It had no message for me. I leaned back against the vinyl booth.

"Can we forget about it for a while?" I said.

"Sure." Stephen crumpled the napkin and punted it to the floor with his fingers. "What's the matter?" he asked.

"I've been thinking," I said. "Maybe this is a bad idea."

"What?"

"This," I said. "Us."

"Oh," said Stephen. "Why?"

"I just feel like I should get through this myself. I mean I think I should pass calculus by myself and then we can decide if we want to see each other."

"But you can't pass calculus by yourself. You need a tutor."

"I'll get another tutor," I said.

"It's too late to get another tutor. We just have one more week. Julie, you know, no one expects you to pass calculus yourself. It's not some big deal. This isn't the Girl Scout merit-badge contest."

"I know," I said. "I can't explain. I just think this is wrong."

Stephen drained his beer glass. "Why won't you let me help you?" he asked.

"I told you," I said. "I think it's wrong."

"But it's not wrong. There's nothing wrong about it. You just want to get rid of me."

I didn't say anything. I watched the cat. We sat there for a moment. I felt like I was making a terrible mistake, only I wasn't sure what it was: if it had to do with love or calculus. I felt I was probably losing on both counts.

I don't think I've worked at anything as hard as I worked at calculus the next week. The exam was scheduled for one o'clock on the last Friday of class; we had a review session in the morning. I asked two questions. Stephen answered them.

I was sitting on the front steps of the math building rereading my notes when he came out. He stood beside me. "Come on," he said. "I'm taking you out to lunch."

"I can't," I said. "I have to study."

He leaned over and pulled my spiral notebook out of my hands. "If you don't know it now," he said, "you never will."

We went across the street to the bar with the slinking white cat. We had a nice lunch. We didn't mention calculus.

I finished the exam before the allotted time was up, which I thought might be a good sign. I couldn't tell. I had no idea how I did. I handed it in and took the subway home. I showered and began packing, because I was going up to the lake to see my parents for the weekend. I was just going out the door when the phone rang. I debated answering it. Most of the calls were still for Alyssa, and I had turned the answering machine on. But it's hard not to answer a ringing phone.

It was Stephen, telling me I had failed the exam and, consequently, the course. For a second I was actually shocked, and then I realized how absurd the whole thing was, my ever thinking I could pass calculus, get an MBA, live in New York. I stood for a moment looking at Alyssa's ridiculous accumulation of crystal. I couldn't speak.

"Julie?" Stephen said. "Are you listening?"

"Yes," I said.

"Listen," he said. "I explained the situation to Foster." Foster was the chairman of the department and a dean at the business school. His eleven-year-old daughter sat next to me in class. She was taking calculus, she told me, for fun.

"You explained the situation?"

"I just told him you almost passed—you almost did—and that you needed the grade to start the program."

"What program?" I asked.

"The MBA," Stephen said.

"Oh," I said. "I've changed my mind about that. I'm not getting an MBA."

"What?" said Stephen. "Are you crazy?"

I was starting to cry, so I didn't say anything.

"Julie? What are you talking about? Why don't we go out to dinner and talk about this?"

"I can't," I said. "I'm going up to my parents'."

"Listen," said Stephen. "Are you listening?"

"I'm not deaf, Stephen."

"I'm going down to the registrar. I'm going to register

you for the August session. I don't even teach it, so it will be O.K. We won't talk about it now. But think about it."

I told him I would think about it; I told him I would call him when I got back on Sunday. I hung up. I stood in Alyssa's pantry. I thought, If I were the kind of person who broke things I would break a glass, or maybe several. I thought, Maybe I should break some even though I'm not that type of person. It would be therapeutic. But I didn't break any. It wasn't worth the effort of cleaning it up, which I would have done, immediately.

Then I started thinking about Stephen. I wished he hadn't called me. He must have started grading my exam the moment I left. Now he was going down to the registrar, at this very moment. He was being so nice. It made me feel guilty and selfish and mean.

I ordered two gin-and-tonics at once from the steward because I wanted two drinks and was afraid he wouldn't make it up the aisle twice by the time we got to Syracuse. They tasted great, and after a while even the fields below us looked trustworthy and harmless, as though if we crashed they'd just reach up and hold us as we fell.

My father was waiting in his Army-surplus jeep at the airport. I threw my knapsack in the back and climbed in the front and we took off. It seemed like he was driving a little too quickly down the tree-lined road; the wind seemed to rush past awfully fast. The sun was finally setting but the light lingered all over the sky.

"I failed my exam," I shouted to my father.

"Oh, honey," he shouted back. "Can you take it again?"

"Maybe. I'll see on Monday."

We drove a little farther in silence and then turned

down the dirt road that goes through the woods to the boathouse.

"Your mother's a little upset," my father said, not looking at me.

"Why? What happened?"

"We had a little argument."

Because my parents never argued in front of me, I thought they never argued. "About what?" I asked.

My father sighed and downshifted. "Your mother wants to settle down. She wants to buy a condominium somewhere." He said "condominium" as if it were a carcinogen.

"Oh," I said.

"I like the way we live. I think it's good for us. I think eventually we should think about settling down in one place. But why now? Look at this—" he motioned out at the land that fell away to the lake that lay as still as a mirror between the trees. "A year ago we didn't know this existed," he said. "I just like finding new things. Making new things."

We pulled into the barn where he parked the jeep, but neither of us made a move to get out.

"I hate to tell you this, honey," my father said. "But I just thought you should know. Mom is in bed. She got kind of upset."

"Oh," I said. My poor father. He sat in his jeep, feeling bad.

"Maybe you should go up and talk to her." For the first time he looked at me. There was just enough light left in the barn for me to see the tears, not falling from his eyes, but sitting in them, glistening.

The electricity in the boathouse was limited to the kitchen, so the rest of the house was dark. I climbed the spiral staircase my father had built to the bedroom. My mother was sitting in bed with her hands folded on the quilt she'd made from scraps of dresses she'd sewn for me and my sister when we were little. Whenever I see the quilt, I can picture some of the dresses, although they were all alike: tiny Peter Pan collars, the fronts smocked, skirts puffed out from the waist. I don't know what happened to them. I wish I still had one or two, just to look at. I sat on the other side of the bed.

"Hi," I said. I leaned over and kissed her. She smiled at me, knowing how silly the situation was: her in bed, me coming to her—it was all wrong, all reversed.

"Did Daddy tell you about our disagreement?" she asked.

I said yes.

She looked out the porthole window my father had installed in the crook of the roof, but it was too dark to see anything.

"I'm sorry now I made such a fuss," she said. "It's just that I can't keep doing this. It's not that I don't have the energy or the will. It's just that I can't keep making things and leaving them behind. Does that seem wrong?"

"No," I said. "Of course not."

She looked at me. "Your father loved you kids, adored you, but he was so happy when you went away to school and he retired. We could finally take off and do things and not be tied down, and it was great for a while but now I'm sick of it. I'm sorry but I'm plain sick of it."

I thought, Don't tell me this, don't say any of this. I don't want to know you're unhappy. And then for the second time that day I felt mean and selfish. My mother sighed and looked back out the window.

I stood up. "Do you want anything from downstairs?"

"No, thanks." She turned away from the window, trying to smile. "How was your exam? I forgot all about it."

"O.K.," I said. "I passed."

A month later, I did pass calculus. It was almost easy the second time. I didn't see Stephen very much; he wasn't teaching so he wasn't really around. When we did see each other we felt awkward: without calculus we had little to share, and for all the hours we had spent together, we didn't seem to know each other very well.

That same week, my parents told me they were separating, at least until they could decide upon a way of life that was "mutually enjoyable." I was surprised and a little ashamed to find that I felt more relieved than upset. While I was growing up I had always been so proud of them, and my intact home, but at some point—and I didn't know when—all that had lost its terrible importance.

They finished work on the boathouse and sold it to a movie star. Over Labor Day weekend, my father went off to Maine to look for a very dilapidated, very large farm. My mother came to see me in New York. We went out to dinner and celebrated my passing calculus. My mother waited until the bottle of champagne was empty and we were drinking brewed decaffeinated coffee before she talked about the separation.

"I feel very brave doing this," she said. "I feel foolish, too, but I do feel brave. And it's nice that it can end like this, with no hard feelings. We really do understand each other. Of course it helps that it's a very specific problem —not something about how we feel about each other."

"But doesn't that make it harder?"

"What?"

"Still feeling the same," I said. "I mean, I'd think if you hated each other it would be easier."

My mother stroked the tablecloth, forming and then smoothing wrinkles. Her hands were covered with tiny cuts and scratches, and I noticed she was still wearing her wedding ring.

"No," she said. "Although I don't know why. I guess I like to think things have changed more than failed. I don't know. Does that make any sense?"

"Yes," I said.

"Debbie doesn't understand at all. She's worried about me. She wants me to move to Allentown."

"What are you going to do?" I asked.

She opened her pocketbook and took out a brochure for condominiums on a golf course in South Carolina. There were pictures of buildings nestled in the rough along green fairways, and floor plans of different models.

"No two are alike," my mother said. "I'm going down next week to look at them."

"They look nice," I said.

"The best thing about them is that I can pick out everything myself: the carpeting, the drapes, the Congoleum, the Formica, the appliances—even the shelf paper."

"That's great." I said. There was a moment when I thought my mother was about to start crying, so I studied the brochure. When I looked up, she seemed O.K.

"And they do all the work," my mother said. "Everything. They even fill the ice trays before you move in."

My mother left for South Carolina on Tuesday, and Wednesday was registration for the fall semester of business school. For a few panic-stricken moments at breakfast, I thought about not going—about getting out of New

York while I was ahead. I could go down and help my mother move into her condominium. But that morning I realized that if I went uptown and registered for accounting and statistics and behavioral management and whatever else, I'd be done with all these second thoughts.

It hasn't been quite like that, of course, but it hasn't been bad. Sometimes I see Stephen around in the late afternoon, and we go across the street to our bar. Now it gets dark while we sit there, but it's still nice. Stephen always asks me if I need help. I tell him no. After the ordeal of calculus, business school is manageable.

⤙⤙⤙ Freddie's Haircut ➤➤➤

"What is it about your life you don't like? What is it you want to change?" Drew, Freddie's roommate, was in the bathroom, talking to Joan, the cat. Freddie went in and sat on the sink. Drew was sitting on the closed toilet, and Joan was crouching in the litterbox. Recently, she had taken to spending most of her time in the litterbox, leaving it only to eat or occasionally watch the traffic on Avenue A.

"We love you, Joan," Drew continued. Joan looked up at them suspiciously and raked the litter with her tail. "Be careful," Drew said to Freddie. "The sink might break." Freddie sat on the rim of the bathtub. "She's been in there all night," Drew said. "I don't understand it. I'm trying to talk her through it."

"Come on, Joan," Freddie offered. "Lighten up."

"You better get out of there soon," Drew said. "If you think I'm going to tolerate this behavior you're crazy."

"Maybe she is crazy," said Freddie. "Maybe she's been inside too long. Cabin fever."

Drew prodded Joan with his bare foot. She leapt out of

the box, spraying gravel, and ran into the hall closet. Freddie began to brush his teeth.

"What are you doing tonight?" Drew said. Drew worked from ten at night to six in the morning in a record store that was open twenty-four hours a day. He had been held up twice. Once the cash register deflected a bullet he claims would have killed him. During the day he went to the New York Restaurant School. The only time Freddie saw him was first thing in the morning.

Freddie looked in the mirror. He appeared rabid. "I'm thinking about getting my ear pierced."

"Why?"

"Why not?" said Freddie. "To look cool. I think it looks cool."

"Mine got infected," Drew said. "Get it done right."

"There's nothing else to do," said Freddie. He spread some Ultra Brite on his front teeth with his middle finger. He hoped this would make them gleam.

Freddie worked for a textile company that specialized in reproducing discontinued fabrics. That afternoon he was standing by the elevators watching the envelopes fall down the mail chute. They dropped as quickly as birds shot from the sky. In a few minutes he could push the down button and go home.

Mrs. Grimes, the office manager, opened the glass lobby doors and said, "Freddie, can I see you in my office before you leave?" Mrs. Grimes's first name was Bernice but she pronounced it Berenice. Freddie had heard her answer the phone.

"Now?" said Freddie.

"In a minute," she said. "What are you doing out here?"

"Someone said a letter was stuck. I was checking it out."

Mrs. Grimes looked disapprovingly at the mail chute. Then she looked disapprovingly at Freddie's new cowboy boots. Then she went back into the lobby.

Mrs. Grimes's office was on the twenty-fourth floor, and by the time Freddie arrived—via the spiral staircase reserved for executives—she was sitting behind her desk, energetically pushing the buttons on a calculator. Her long fingernails prevented her from expending her total fury. "Sit down," she said, without looking up.

The only chair was occupied by Mrs. Grimes's dachshund-shaped handbag. Freddie was afraid to move it.

"Sit down," Mrs. Grimes repeated, this time looking up.

Freddie picked up the handbag and sat with it on his lap. Then he put it on the floor.

"I see nothing to be except frank," Mrs. Grimes began, confusing Freddie immediately. "Are you stealing blue Uni-ball pens?"

Freddie was the supply distributor for the twenty-fifth floor. He had stolen a stapler and a Rolodex for the apartment, but he had stolen no pens. "No," he said.

"I ask because, according to my information, several gross are missing."

Since Freddie wasn't sure how many were involved in a gross, he couldn't tell how grave the situation was. "I haven't taken any," he said. "I don't need pens."

"You could sell them," Mrs. Grimes suggested.

Freddie shrugged.

"Do you lock your closet whenever you vacate it?"

"Yes," Freddie lied.

"Then I am afraid the blame must be yours. I will let

it pass this time, but I will keep a close watch on the comings and goings of pens on the twenty-fifth floor. And I will not hesitate to charge any further losses against your paycheck."

"O.K.," Freddie said. He stood up and put the handbag on the chair. It rolled to its side and a pack of cigarettes fell on the floor. Freddie leaned down and picked them up.

"Leave them," Mrs. Grimes said. "Don't touch them."

A girl who looked about thirteen sat behind a glass case filled with earrings and roach clips, reading *Interview* magazine. Freddie looked in the case. Some of the earrings looked like they were made out of tabs from beer cans.

"Can I help you?" the girl asked.

"I think so," said Freddie. He sat down on a stool.

"We close at eleven," the girl said, although it was only a little after ten.

"I want an ear pierced," Freddie said. "Just one."

"You'll have to pay for two. It's a flat rate."

"O.K.," Freddie said.

"Pain or no pain?" the girl asked.

"Are you serious?"

"Yes," the girl said. She picked up an apparatus that looked like the embosser Freddie's mother used to personalize her stationery. "Some people like the pain. It makes the experience more real. It's not that bad."

"I want no pain," Freddie said.

"O.K.," the girl said. She went in the back of the store and returned with an ice cube. It was already beginning to melt in her palm. "Which ear?" she asked.

"Oh," said Freddie. "I'm not sure."

"Are you gay?"

"No," said Freddie.

"Then the right one. Left means you're gay."

"Are you sure?"

"Of course," said the girl. "Here. Hold this against your lobe till it melts."

Freddie held the ice cube against his right ear lobe. "Do I get to pick out the earring?"

"No," said the girl. "You have to have a fourteen-karat gold stud."

"Is that included?"

"No. It's fifteen dollars. I can give you just one for ten."

"So it's fourteen dollars altogether?" Freddie asked. His cheek was getting wet from the melting ice.

The girl nodded. "Is that melted yet?"

Freddie held up the thin disk of ice.

"A few more minutes," she said. She opened a bottle of rubbing alcohol and took a cotton ball out of a plastic bag. "I could put two holes in one ear," she said. "That looks good."

"Can I take it out?" Freddie asked.

"Not for six weeks. Otherwise your hole closes."

The ice slivered out of Freddie's hand and fell to the floor. He wiped his wet fingers on his pants.

"O.K.," the girl said. "One or two?"

"One," said Freddie.

She motioned for him to lean forward and wiped his ear with the cotton ball. Then she fingered his lobe and said, "Can you feel this?"

"No," Freddie said. The girl lifted the piercer and rested her hand against Freddie's cheek, steadying his head with her other hand. Freddie felt like he was being comforted. He closed his eyes, and felt his lashes scrape against the girl's throat.

* * *

No one noticed—or commented on—Freddie's earring until he went home for his sister's graduation-from-midwifery-school party. It was Freddie's idea to cut a sheet cake in the form of a baby and cover it with flesh-colored frosting. He was surrounded by chunks of cake and puddles of food coloring. The baby kept getting smaller and smaller. His mother was spraying rosettes of cheese food from an aerosol can onto crackers. "I've tried not to notice that thing in your ear," she said. "Is it really an earring?"

"It is," said Freddie.

"What does it mean? Or would I rather not know?"

"It doesn't mean anything," Freddie said. He touched the tiny stud, coating it with pink frosting.

"First gypsies wore earrings," said his mother. "Then Catholics. Then normal girls. And now my son. Where will it end?"

"With pets," Freddie said.

There was a girl who worked in Deferred Sales whom Freddie liked. He sent her anonymous gifts of unrequisitioned supplies through the mail. On Friday afternoon she opened the supply-closet door and said, "Rumor has it you're the man with the stuff."

Freddie was arranging bottles of liquid paper on a shelf. "Stuff?" he said. "You mean supplies?"

"In a way," she said. "Supplies for living." She closed the door and sat on a stool.

Freddie didn't understand. "Huh?" he said.

The girl opened a bottle of pink liquid paper and began painting her thumbnail. "It's a madhouse out there," she said. "Do you mind if I hang out for a minute?"

"No," said Freddie.

"I'm Diane," the girl said.

"I know," said Freddie.

"What I meant before was, do you have any pot?"

"Who said I had pot?"

"I thought it was common knowledge. I thought people were always escaping to the supply closet to get high."

"Not this one," Freddie said.

Diane observed her pink nail and switched to ledger-green liquid paper.

"I'd check the mailroom," said Freddie. "If you're that desperate."

"I'm not desperate. I'm just a little tense." Diane capped the bottle and fanned her polished nails at arm's length. "I like your cowboy boots," she said. "They're so pointy. Do they hurt?"

"No," Freddie lied.

"You must have weird feet then."

"Do you like my earring?" Freddie asked.

"You have an earring?"

Freddie bared his ear. "No one notices."

"Are you gay?"

"No," said Freddie. "It's the right ear."

"That means you're gay."

"No. It means you're straight."

"If you want people to notice it, you should get your hair cut."

"You think so?" asked Freddie. "How short?"

"I don't know." Diane stood up. "I could cut it for you. Do you have scissors?"

"Of course," said Freddie. "But do you know how?"

"I've done it before. I love to cut people's hair. I cut my boyfriend's." She opened the cabinet. "Where are the scissors?"

Before Freddie could dissuade her, Diane found a pair

of scissors and began to snip them ferociously in the air. "Sit on the stool," she commanded. "I'll just cut a little around the ears."

"Are you sure about this?"

"Don't worry."

Freddie sat on the stool. Diane ran her fingers through his hair. "You have funny hair," she said. "It sticks out funny."

"I didn't wash it this morning," Freddie explained. "We didn't have any hot water."

Diane started snipping. She handed the cut hair to Freddie. Someone knocked on the door.

"Shit," Diane said. She tried to throw the scissors back into the cabinet but they landed on the floor, and separated.

Mrs. Grimes opened the door. Freddie jumped up from the stool, and his cut hair flurried to the floor. All three of them watched it for a second.

"Excuse me," Diane said. "I was just leaving."

Mrs. Grimes watched Diane leave. "I see you've been getting a haircut, Freddie," she said.

"I guess so," said Freddie.

"I think I should like to see you in my office before you leave today."

"O.K.," said Freddie.

Mrs. Grimes went out and closed the door. Freddie picked up his cut hair and put it in an inter-office envelope. He sent it to Diane.

Drew was whipping egg whites with a rat-tail comb when Freddie got home. He looked at Freddie's head and said, "What happened?"

"Everything," said Freddie.

"No. Really. What happened to your hair?"

"It got cut. At least some of it. And I got fired."

"You got fired? Why?"

"For getting my hair cut," said Freddie.

"They can't fire you for being ugly, can they?"

"Thanks," said Freddie. "That's just what I needed to hear. No, this girl was cutting my hair in the closet and the office manager found us."

"And she fired you?"

"Yeah," said Freddie.

"She fired you because you were getting your hair cut?"

"She also thought I was stealing pens."

"Were you?"

"No," said Freddie.

"You need a drink," said Drew. He inserted the comb into the meringue and watched to see if it would stand. It did. "Let me fix you a drink."

Drew mixed some vodka with some Cranapple juice and gave it to Freddie. Freddie drank it. "What am I going to do?" he said.

"It'll all work out," Drew said. "But I'd get my hair fixed before I look for another job."

After Drew left for work Freddie took a shower and washed his hair. It didn't look much better clean. He was trying to decide if he could fix it himself when the phone rang. It always seemed to ring when Freddie was naked.

"Hello," he said.

"Hi," said his mother. "This is me."

"Hi," said Freddie.

"What's the matter?"

"Nothing."

"Oh," said his mother. "I was calling to see if you got the check."

"What check?" asked Freddie.

"The check I sent you. You didn't get it?"

"No," said Freddie. "Not yet."

"Well, I thought you could use a little extra money. It's just for fifteen dollars."

"Thanks," said Freddie.

"What are you doing?"

"Nothing. I might go out and get my hair cut later."

"Isn't it too late for that?"

"Some places around here are open late. Till midnight."

"How's work?"

"O.K.," said Freddie.

"Monica delivered her first official baby today."

"Oh," said Freddie. "How did it go?"

"Fine, I guess. She said it was a little difficult because the woman insisted on having it in the dark. I think it's absurd: having your baby at home in bed with all the lights out."

"It's the new thing," said Freddie. "It's supposed to be better for the baby."

"You were born in an operating room. I don't remember anything. The last thing I remember is lying on the couch timing the pains and watching a war movie. All these planes flying back and forth, back and forth. I forget the rest."

Freddie couldn't think of what to say. He wanted to say, "I got fired," but it was all too complicated and horrible to admit. "I've got to go," he said.

"I'll talk to you soon," said his mother. "I hope you get a nice haircut. Freddie?"

"What?"

"I'm sorry about what I said about your earring. I mean, I shouldn't have said it. I think it's fine for you to have an earring. Really, I do. I hope I didn't upset you."

"No," said Freddie.

"O.K., honey. Bye-bye."

"Bye," said Freddie.

There were two people in the haircutting place when Freddie arrived. A woman was sitting in one of the chairs watching herself drink coffee from a paper cup in the mirror. It was as if she were watching TV and starring on it at the same time. A man with a zebra-striped mohawk was sweeping the cut hair on the floor into a pile. Freddie stood inside the door.

Finally the woman turned away from the mirror and said, "Do you want your hair cut or something?"

"Yes," said Freddie.

She got out of the chair and motioned for Freddie to take her place. He did.

The woman took a comb out of a jar of blue liquid and poked Freddie's head. "It looks like it's just been cut," she said.

"It was a mistake," said Freddie. "Can you fix it?"

"Sure," the woman said.

"I want it cut the way it is now, only a little shorter."

"No you don't," the woman said. "We'll fix it up."

"How?" asked Freddie.

"Trust me," the woman said. She opened a drawer and removed a set of hedge clippers.

"What are they?" asked Freddie.

"They're shears," said the woman. "They give your hair a lot more texture. And height."

"Oh," said Freddie.

The woman tousled Freddie's hair and attacked it with the shears, snipping randomly at the tufted locks. "I'm cutting on the angle," she said. "To add fullness."

Freddie watched in the mirror, fascinated. Even the skunk-like man laid down his broom and watched. The woman tousled with one hand and snipped with the other, establishing a rhythm that was oddly soothing for all its fury. Freddie felt like he was outside, hatless, in a terrible storm.

He did not cry until he got home. He managed to pay the woman—even tip her—and walk home, all the time hoping that his hair would look better in his own, familiar mirror.

He went into the dark bathroom and could sense Joan crouching in the litterbox. Freddie knew why she was there. One day she was sitting on the window sill, watching the traffic while he was washing dishes. He dropped a plate, and as it shattered, he heard Joan screech, and when he looked up, the window sill was empty. He ran downstairs—two flights—and found her, stunned but alive, flattened against the sidewalk. He carried her upstairs, and ever since then she crouched near to the floor in small, contained places. Freddie doesn't know why he feels responsible for this. Technically, it was an accident.

When he turned on the bathroom light and saw himself in the mirror his worst fears were confirmed. His spiky hair looked menacing and hideous, and as he leaned toward his reflection it occurred to him that even he, even now, did not deserve to look this ugly.

At my little sister Missie's wedding, there were flowers at the end of every pew, six bridesmaids and six ushers, a reception in our backyard with a yellow-and-white-striped tent, and a dance floor built over the swimming pool. My boyfriend, Carl, got so drunk he chased me into the garage and told me, in between the Audi and the station wagon, that he would never, ever marry me. Then, in a desperate and embarrassing gesture, he snapped the antenna of the Audi and handed it to me, apologetically, like a gift.

To get away from Carl, I went upstairs to Missie's and my old bedroom. A woman I didn't recognize was lying on one of the twin beds, surrounded by Missie's dolls from many lands. I sat on the other bed.

"Were you a bridesmaid?" the woman asked.

"Maid of honor," I said.

I looked at my dress and decided to take it off. Missie's going-away outfit was laid out on the bed as if she had died in it and been carefully extracted. I thought about putting that on and leaving myself, but instead I changed into a pair of jeans and a turtleneck with green hearts all over it. The woman watched me change.

"I was having a little lie-down," she said. She sat up and smoothed her skirt. I was trying to decide if I knew her or remembered her from the receiving line. When Carl had come through the line, he had kissed my hand and whispered that I was ten million times more beautiful than the bride. That was before he got drunk.

"I think they're cutting the cake," I said. "If you want a piece, you better go."

"They cut it a while ago," the woman said. "I had a piece. I think that's what made me feel so queer."

I looked out the window. Carl was playing touch football on the front lawn with some little kids. His tuxedo was getting all rumpled.

My mother opened the door. "There you are," she said to me. She looked at the woman. "Are you feeling any better, Jane?"

"It's Joan," the woman said. "Not much." She stood in front of the mirror and poked at her hair, which was considerably disheveled; then, apparently satisfied, she walked down the hall.

"Who is that?" I asked.

"I'm not sure," my mother said. "Helen, why did you change? You'll have to change back. The photographer wants us on the front steps waving to departing guests."

"I'd rather die," I said.

"So would we all, darling," said my mother, "but think of Missie."

"I am," I said.

I put my dress back on and went out onto the front steps. Carl was sitting on the football, and Bump, the dog, was trying to chew it out from under him. Bump liked

Carl. The photographer was standing under a tree, looking up through his camera at the sky.

"Finally," he said to me. "Where is everybody else?"

"I don't know," I said.

I sat on the top step. I would never wear the dress again, so it didn't matter if I got it dirty. We had talked about getting sensible dresses we could use again, but Missie vetoed that idea. She wanted them to be special.

Bump nosed the football out from under Carl, who fell over. If I hadn't been mad at him, I would have asked him if he was hurt, or even helped him up, but I just watched him. My father came out the door behind me. He was holding a beer stein in one hand and a cocktail napkin in the other. We had ordered a thousand mauve, pink, and peach napkins with "Melissa & Henry—September 10, 1983" embossed on them. He set the napkin on my head, and then kept his hand there. I knew this was an excuse for touching me, but I didn't mind. The photographer stepped over Carl and said, "Hold it." My father raised his stein in salute, and the photographer took the shot. Carl sat up to watch. Missie appeared through the hedge, practically dragging Hank. They had probably been sharing a joint in the neighbor's pool house. My mother arrived, and the photographer arranged us: Missie and Hank on the lawn, with Missie's long train artfully spread to hide the burned spot on the grass; my mother and father on the first step; and me on the top step, so just my head was visible between their shoulders. Then he told us to shout goodbye and wave, but there was no one there except Carl —all the other guests were out back—so we waved goodbye to him, and the photographer took a picture. My parents used it for their Christmas card.

* * *

The rehearsal dinner, the night before, was at the Rolling River Country Club. My father doesn't play golf—he always works on Saturdays—but Hank's father does, so his family belonged. We had dinner in the Mississippi Room (all the rooms are named after rivers). Women in black dresses with white aprons brought us kiwi fruit cup, chicken with asparagus, and tortoni. They all looked like the mothers of people I had gone to high school with.

The beer came in pitcher after pitcher, and a toast seemed to accompany every one—some sentimental, some obscene. Hank was standing on his chair, his big cheeks flushed, and Missie sat beside him, embarrassed, striking pink-tipped wooden matches. There was something medieval about the scene.

First the old people left, and then the bridal party hung out in the bar, which overlooked the large, lighted swimming pool. We were all drunk and throwing Goldfish crackers up into the air and catching them in our mouths. Hank and his best man periodically went outside and raced around the clubhouse to sober up, and each time they came back they seemed to have shed another article of clothing, till they arrived bare-chested and sweating and we were all asked to leave.

The boys and some of the braver bridesmaids went out to a bar called the Clutch, but Missie wanted to go home, and I was glad to take her. We drove slowly down the narrow road through the golf course, with the fairways stretching out on either side like long, thin lakes. When we got on the main road, we passed a bank that flashed the time and temperature. It was 2:47 and 62°. Missie said, "I can't believe in thirteen hours I'm getting married."

Next to the bank was a Dunkin' Donuts, and as soon

as I saw its pink sign and lighted interior I realized I was
starving. I pulled in and Missie and I sat at the empty,
curving counter. Missie had a cup of tea, and I had coffee
and a butternut doughnut. For a while we said nothing.
I watched the girl in the back room insert a nozzle into
doughnuts and fill them with jelly. She did it very deli-
cately, as if the doughnuts had feelings. It was all so
peaceful, in that way only the very middle of the night is.

Finally Missie said, "What did you think of all that?"
She was picking up the crumbs from my doughnut with
her moistened middle finger.

"You mean the dinner?" I said. "Or the rehearsal?"

"Both," said Missie.

"I think it's a nice service," I said. "I like the traditional
vows. When people make them up they sound so phony."

"I don't know," Missie said.

"About what?"

"About it all," Missie said. "About this whole thing. I
mean, not about getting married. Just how to do it. I'm
afraid if I leave anything out I'll regret it later. I don't want
to be thirty-five and cry because I didn't have a wedding
cake with a bride and groom on top. Or a book for guests
to sign. But now I really don't know."

Even though I thought you would probably regret the
things you did more than the things you didn't do, I said,
"I went to a wedding where they had carrot cake instead
of wedding cake. It was a joke. The frosting had raisins
in it, and it looked all lumpy."

Missie took a linen napkin out of her coat pocket and
opened it on the counter. Inside there were two jumbo
shrimps. "I stole these from the sushi bar at the dinner,"
Missie said. "I felt like I should keep them to show my
children or something. Or freeze them and eat them on

our anniversary." The shrimp were already turning tan and hard. Missie poked one of them. "This is really stupid," she said. "Let's get out of here."

We got up and left, and as I started the car I saw the girl come and clear our things. She didn't look twice at the shrimp; she just dumped them in the bucket with our mugs and crumbs and lemon rind. I hoped Missie hadn't seen.

Carl and I had planned to stay overnight after the wedding, but we didn't. After the last guest left, I found him fast asleep in the Cougar we had rented to drive down to Jersey the day before. I had gone to the car, which was parked halfway up the street, to get my special present for Missie: antique earrings I had bought in SoHo. I forgot to give them to her before the wedding, and now it would have to wait—she and Hank had driven off in the limo an hour ago. They were staying at the Holiday Inn at Newark Airport and flying to St. John in the morning. I sat in the passenger seat and looked at the earrings and thought about keeping them for myself, but they were for Missie, and I wanted her to have them. Or rather, I wanted to give them to her. The summer Missie started seeing Hank, I had said a very mean thing about him. Hank was the state champion pole-vaulter, and Missie took me to a track meet to watch him jump. While all the other athletes ran around and stretched and threw things, Hank lay on the crash mats with his shirt off, sunbathing. When it came time for him to jump, he jumped higher than anyone else, but later he told me it was all technique and didn't really require much practice once it had been mastered. He chewed tobacco and spat. I called him a lazy slob, and it was one of those things everyone pretends to forget but remembers. So it was nice of Missie to ask me to be maid of honor, even if she did ask our other sister, Cara, first. That made sense because Cara is closer in age to Missie. Unfortunately, she was spending a semester in Alaska and couldn't come home. She sent a postcard of an Eskimo couple standing outside their igloo.

When I looked up I saw Mr. Chatto walking his Great Dane, Sheba, along the street. It was his house we were parked in front of. We didn't know him very well, and he hadn't been invited to the wedding. Since all the guests had left, the Cougar was parked all by itself at his curb in the dark, and Mr. Chatto came over and looked in the open window. So did Sheba.

"Hello," I said.

"Ah, good evening," Mr. Chatto said. "How was the wedding?"

"Fine," I said.

Carl woke up with a lurch in the back seat. He surprised Mr. Chatto, and Sheba, who barked. "Where are we?" he asked. He thought we had been driving.

"Right here," I said. "We haven't moved."

"Good night," Mr. Chatto said.

"What are we doing in the car?" Carl asked.

"Nothing," I said. "Hanging out."

"What time is it?"

"About ten," I said. "I don't know."

Carl untucked his shirt and then tucked it back into his pants. His cummerbund had come undone, and he picked it up off the floor of the car. He tried to climb into the front seat but bumped his head on the ceiling. "Ow," he said. I laughed.

Carl opened the door and stood on Mr. Chatto's front lawn. "It's kind of nice out here," he said. "It's quiet."

I didn't say anything. I held the pearl earrings against my ears and looked at myself in the rearview mirror. One of Missie's dumb friends had offered to do the makeup on the bridal party as a wedding present. She put a ton of makeup on me, and it was all smudging or worn off. I looked a mess.

Carl leaned in through the open window and rested his head on his hands, so that the top of his head almost touched my shoulder. "Helen, what I said," he whispered. "About marrying you. I'm sorry."

"It's O.K.," I said. I threw the earrings over his head onto Mr. Chatto's lawn. It was for effect only: I made sure I marked the spots where they landed. "I never said I wanted to get married."

"I thought you did."

"I don't want to talk about it."

"Are you drunk?" Carl asked. "Because if you are we shouldn't be having such a serious discussion. We should wait."

"I'm not drunk," I said.

"I am." He looked down at the street. Mr. Chatto turned on the large-screen TV in his living room, and the whole room glowed. "So do you want to get married?" Carl said to his feet.

"I thought we weren't going to talk about this now," I said.

"I meant if we were both drunk. You said you weren't."

"Oh, you can talk about it when you're drunk, but I can't."

"No," Carl said. He leaned his head back in through the car window. "I meant that since this was an important discussion, one of us should be sober. To remember what we say. If we're both drunk, we shouldn't waste our time."

I wasn't sure what to say.

"But this is really ideal," Carl continued. "I'm always more honest when I'm drunk."

"Good," I said. "Be honest."

"About what?"

"About me. About us."

"Maybe I'm just scared," Carl said. "Maybe we should get married. I mean, Missie and Hank—"

I touched his head to shut him up. He had slicked his hair back with Tenax, so his forehead was smooth and exposed and warm, and with my palm on it I tilted his head so I could look at his face. "Will you get my earrings?"

"What?"

"I threw them out the window. Missie's earrings."

"Where are they?"

"One is by the mailbox and one is by the little dwarf. The statue."

Carl straightened up and I directed. "You're getting warmer," I said as he walked toward the mailbox. "You're hot. You're burning. You're on fire."

When I went inside to get our stuff, I found my father asleep on the living-room couch. The TV was on, but the sound was turned very low. It was *Fantasy Island.* I turned it off.

"Hey," my father said. "I was watching that."

I made no move to turn the set back on, and neither did he. I shifted some wedding presents from the love seat onto the floor and sat down. "Where's Mom?" I asked.

"She's taking a bath," my father said. "Where's the Prince?" For some reason I don't particularly care to know, my father has always called Carl the Prince.

"He's taking a walk," I said. "To sober up. We're going back tonight."

"Does he always get that looped?"

"Only at weddings," I said. "And cocktail parties."

"I met your mother at a cocktail party. She was wearing a cocktail dress. She was drinking a cocktail. I was looped."

"I met Carl at a fraternity party," I said. "He was wearing a toga and drinking beer from a plastic cup."

"I'd pick your mother any day," my father said.

The phone rang. I went into the kitchen and answered it.

"Oh, God," Missie said. "This is me."

"Missie," I said. "What's the matter?"

"I forgot my contacts sterilizer. I can't take them out without it. Could you bring it over?"

"I guess so," I said. "Where is it?"

"I'm not sure. Mom might know. I thought I packed it."

"We'll drop it off on our way back. We're leaving in a little while. What floor are you on?"

"I have no idea," Missie said. "It's up high. Ask at the desk."

"What are you doing?" I asked. "How's married life?"

"O.K.," said Missie. "But my eyes are burning. Hank is taking a sauna. There's one in the bathroom. He's never had one before."

"You should take one together," I said. "It's your wedding night."

"I can't unless I take my contacts out," Missie said. "They melt or something."

"Do you want to talk to Mom?"

"God, no," Missie said.

"O.K.," I said. "We'll be over around midnight."

"Thanks," said Missie. "See ya."

I hung up the phone. My mother came into the kitchen, fresh from her bath. She was wearing a robe and had a towel wrapped around her head like a turban. When I try to do that, the towel unwinds every time I move my head. My mother can do aerobics and keep the towel intact. She is very beautiful. She is always playing countesses at the local dinner theater. She sat down at the kitchen table and looked at her reflection in the dark kitchen window.

"I better go find Carl," I said. "He's taking a walk. We're leaving."

"Oh," my mother said. She rested her hands, palm down, on the table and studied her nails. She had had them manicured and painted to match her peach-colored dress for the wedding, but the polish was already gone. I'm sure she did it sitting in her bath with the cotton balls and nail-polish remover carefully arranged on the portable vanity table that stretches across the tub. I was irked that she had already stripped her nails. If I had peach nails for my daughter's wedding, I would have let the polish chip off, little by little, for days.

The sign outside the Holiday Inn said WELCOME POLAR BEARS. It didn't mention Missie and Hank. I parked the car. "Do you want to come in?" I asked Carl.

"No," he said. "I've had enough of Missie and Hank for one day."

"O.K., I'll be right back." I went into the lobby, holding Missie's sterilizer. She was sitting on a couch there, reading *People*.

"Missie!" I said. "What are you doing down here? I was going to bring it up."

"Hank-o's asleep," Missie said. "He's had a rough day. And the sauna kind of exhausted him."

"Oh," I said. I had had visions of creeping down a long, quiet hallway and knocking on the door of the bridal suite, leaving the sterilizer outside, and running back to the elevator. I had visions of Missie opening the door in her wedding gown or a negligee. I wasn't prepared to find her sitting in the lobby in jeans and T-shirt. I still had on my bridesmaid dress, and I felt as if I was the only one left who had anything to do with the wedding. "Do you want to get a drink?" I asked Missie. "There must be a bar in here."

"I'm tired," said Missie. "We have to get up at six-thirty."

"I feel like going dancing," I said.

"Go dancing," Missie said.

"But it's your wedding," I said. "Don't you want to do something fun?"

"Helen," said Missie, "I want to go to bed, O.K.?" She pushed the button for the elevator. "I want to take my contacts out. That's all I really want to do."

The elevator doors opened and Missie got in, and I realized I still hadn't given her the pearl earrings. "Wait right here," I said. "I have a present for you. I'll be right back."

I ran out to the car to get the earrings. Carl was asleep, or pretending to be.

In the lobby, Missie was still standing in the elevator, holding the door open with her hand. I noticed her ring for the first time.

"Here," I said. I handed Missie the earrings.

She opened the tissue wrapping and looked at them. "Thanks," she said. "They're really pretty."

"They're antiques," I said.

"Why are you giving them to me?" Missie asked. "Do you feel sorry for me?"

"No," I said. "I feel happy for you. I'm happy for you."

"Oh," said Missie. "I wasn't sure. I feel like everyone's sorry for me."

"Well, isn't it a little anticlimactic?" I asked. The elevator alarm started buzzing, and Missie stepped out. The doors closed. "I mean, aren't you sorry it's all over?"

"No," said Missie. "I'm happy. I wish you'd stop feeling sorry for me."

"I don't feel sorry for you," I said. "I just told you that."

"Helen?"

"What?"

"What do you think about Hank? Do you still think he's a jerk?"

I didn't know what to say. I pushed the elevator button and the door opened. It had gone nowhere.

"Tell me," Missie said. "I want to know."

"No," I said. "I think he's nice."

"You think he's nice?"

"Well, you know," I said. "He's not really my type."

"He's like Carl," Missie said.

"No, he's not," I said. "At least I don't think so." And this was true—there were a million things about Carl that weren't at all like Hank. Hank wore white socks with loafers, and T-shirts were always visible at his open collar. He took Missie to see *Fanny and Alexander* because he thought it was Ingrid Bergman's last movie, and left halfway through. Of course, there are other, nice things about Hank. He's just not like Carl.

"I like Hank a lot," Missie said. The elevator door started to close, and Missie tried and failed to hold it open. It knocked one of the earrings out of her hand and down the crack into the void. "Oh, God," Missie said. She started to cry.

"Missie," I said. "What's wrong?"

"I don't know," Missie said. She rested her arms along the wall and hid her face against them. I patted her on the back. Her hair was still full of hair spray from her bridal hairdo, and every time she gulped it all moved at once, like a wig. A woman wearing a fur coat and slippers came through the lobby doors walking a cat in a harness and stood beside us. The cat had a little crystal necklace on.

"I better go up," Missie said. She had stopped crying.

"Are you sure you're all right?"

"I'm just tired," Missie said. "Please don't tell Mom, O.K.?"

"Of course not," I said.

Missie looked at her remaining earring. "If they don't find it, I'll get a second hole in one ear," she said. "I can wear it with my jade studs."

"That would look pretty," I said.

The elevator door opened, and the woman and the cat and Missie got in. The woman picked up the cat and pushed her floor button with the cat's small paw.

The doors closed, and I stood in the lobby for a moment. I remembered this afternoon, and Missie walking down the aisle. I went first, and Missie and my father waited until I was all the way in the sanctuary before they began. I turned around and watched them. It seemed to take them forever to march past all those upraised, weeping faces, and I remembered thinking it was more like climbing up a hill than walking down an aisle—meeting someone, getting him to call you, kissing him, falling in love with him, sleeping with him, getting engaged, shopping in a bridal mall, choosing the band and the caterer, losing weight to fit the dress, opening the wedding presents, sitting through the rehearsal dinner, waking up in the morning knowing you were going to be married that day. All these things seemed like little plateaus on some mountain Missie had climbed during the past year, and as I saw her get closer I realized I didn't want her to arrive at the top. I felt scared for myself up there—scared that in all that wind and silence and love I'd lose my balance or blow away. Even the air seemed insubstantial and strangely cool. I was glad when it was all over and we stood outside the church, our backs to the traffic, laughing.

When I came out of the hotel, a plane passed so close I saw faces in the tiny lighted windows. Carl had pulled the car up outside the door and was waiting with the engine running. I was glad he had waked up, for I was in no mood to drive home in silence. I could hardly wait until we got out on the highway. We'd put the top down and turn the radio up loud, and speed.

What Do People Do All Day?

Guess what my monogram is," asks Mark. He is sitting at the porch table eating a bowl of Froot Loops: first the pink, then the yellow, and finally the orange circles. The bowl keeps changing color.

Diane, the babysitter, watches him put a yellow spoonful into his mouth. She is not babysitting for him but for his stepbrother, Will, who is sitting in his high chair watching TV.

"Your monogram?" Diane asks. She has the feeling that Mark is smarter than she is and that his questions have some tricky double meaning.

"My monogram. You know, like on a sweater or something. My initials."

"Well," says Diane. "M for Mark and V for Volkenburg. What's your middle name?"

"Theodore," says Mark. "For Daddy. Get it?"

"What?" admits Diane, feeling dense.

"MTV," says Mark. "M—T—V. Like on cable TV."

"Oh," says Diane. She gives the baby a spoonful of the peaches and yogurt his mother, Helen—Mark's step-mother—had blended that morning. Will allows the tiny leaf-shaped spoon to be inserted into his mouth, but makes no attempt to swallow the pale orange mush. It slides out of his mouth. Mark watches and imitates with yellow, partly chewed Froot Loops.

Helen is a lawyer and works in the city part-time. Diane comes at eight and leaves whenever Helen or Ted, her husband, comes home. Ted, a recently untenured communications professor at Drew, is now looking for work in the "real world": television, cable TV, video. He is having no luck.

Outside the screen windows, in the kidney-shaped swimming pool, Annette is swimming her thirtieth, and final, lap. Annette is Mark's mother—Ted's first wife. She lives around the block and every morning, when she sees Helen's car drive past on the way to the bus stop, she pulls her jogging suit on over her bathing suit, trots through the backyards, and dives into her ex-husband's pool. Technically, she is not allowed to do this. She has Mark all of July and every other week during the school year, but thirty—hopefully fifty by the end of the summer—laps never hurt anyone, especially since she does them when Helen and Ted are out. They never use the pool anyway. Diane and Mark are sworn to secrecy.

Annette gets out of the pool, panting, and dries herself with a towel left out overnight, then wraps it around her waist skirtlike and opens the porch door.

"How many?" Mark asks.

"Three O," Annette says. "What's that?" She nods at Mark's cereal. "Lunch?"

"Breakfast," says Mark. "Froot Loops."

"No wonder you like it here," Annette says. "They let you eat junk."

"It's vitamin fortified," Mark says. "See." He holds up the cereal box.

Annette ignores the box but picks some green grapes from the fruit bowl. She doesn't seem to notice that she is dripping water on the floor. Diane watches, fascinated. She is intrigued with Annette. She hasn't figured her out yet.

"How's Gerber?" Annette asks the baby. She calls him Gerber because she thinks he looks like the Gerber baby. She always makes it sound like an insult, although secretly she is jealous of how beautiful Will is. Mark was kind of an ugly baby.

"Gerber doesn't like this yogurt," Diane says.

"Let me try it," Annette says. She takes the baby spoon from the Peter Rabbit porringer and tastes the puréed peaches. "It's good," she says. "We should all eat this well."

Diane pulls Will out of the high chair, takes off his sodden bib and sits him on the floor. "He needs to be changed," she announces.

"That's your job," says Annette. "At least you get paid for it. I never got paid for it. I did it for love. For my little poppet." She reaches out and tousles Mark's hair, which is already tufted from sleep.

"I'm not your little puppet," says Mark. He eats the last orange Froot Loop.

"You were," says Annette.

"No," says Mark, "I wasn't."

"Oh, but you were, darling. You used to beg me to call you poppet. You would beg me—when you were as little as Gerber."

"He can't talk," says Mark. "So I couldn't have begged

you." He drinks the sweet pastel-colored milk from the bowl. Annette watches him.

"You could talk," she says. "You were very smart. Very advanced." She gets up and opens the refrigerator. "When does she come home today?" she asks Diane.

"She's taking the one-thirty bus."

"Does that mean it leaves or arrives at one-thirty?" Annette takes a swig from a bottle of seltzer, then puts it back in the refrigerator. She enjoys the thought of her spittle mixed, unknowingly, with Ted's. He taught her to drink seltzer from the bottle.

"It leaves at one-thirty," says Diane. She picks up Will. "It gets here at two-forty."

"Good," says Annette. She closes the refrigerator. "That gives me the peak hours by the pool."

"What are the peak hours?" asks Mark.

"Prime Time Tanning Hours," says Annette. "Sun Ray City. Eleven A.M. to two P.M."

The "employment counselor" suggested from the start that Ted shave his beard, but he resisted. He likes his beard. He's had it for a long time. Originally, it was all black, but now it's streaked with silver—silver, not white. At least the half of it that is still on his face.

It is noon and Ted is at his friend's apartment in the city, shaving off his beard. He is between "sessions." Everything in job hunting has an unexpected name: "sessions" instead of interviews, "networking" instead of socializing. Barbara Brown, his counselor, is wonderfully maternal: she gets him coffee every morning for their "strategy meetings," gives him quarters so he can call her from the street "first thing" after every session and "report back in." He will miss her, if he ever finds a job. Ted looks at his half-shaved face in the mirror. Maybe he should stop now and get a job in a circus: half man, half woman. He tries to smile with one half of his face and frown with the other. Then he continues shaving, making long sweeps with the razor he just bought, letting the moist curls of hair fall from the razor down his arms and into the sink. His mouth, uncovered, looks all wrong.

Helen never worries that Will will get hurt or get sick or die. She worries that he will forget her; that he will look up at her—from his crib, if he's napping, from his high chair, if he's having a snack, or from Diane's arms—not with the wonderful smile of recognition he has recently acquired but with a dumb, vacant stare. Sometimes, too, riding home on the bus in the afternoon, she has trouble picturing Will. It upsets her that she cannot commit his tiny body to memory. Perhaps it is because he is changing so quickly. He does look slightly different every afternoon.

This afternoon when she gets home everyone is in the pool. Will has his swimmies on and Mark and Diane are pushing him back and forth. Will is laughing, but when he sees Helen he raises his fists in the air, clutching and unclutching them. Helen pulls him out of the pool, and holds him, even though he is all wet.

Diane climbs out and pours a glass of water over her head. Helen watches her comb out her long blond hair.

"Why did you do that?" she asks.

"It's seltzer," Diane says. "It rinses the chlorine out."

"Oh," says Helen.

"Can I do that?" asks Mark.

"Sure," says Helen.

Mark gets out of the pool and pours his glass over his head. Scarlet juice drips down his face.

"You don't do it with cranberry juice, dummy," Diane says.

Mark licks his lips and his shoulders, then jumps in the pool. The water around him turns pink, but quickly clears.

"Did Ted call?" Helen asks.

"Yes," says Diane.

"What did he say?"

"He probably won't be home for dinner. Don't count on him."

The receptionist tells Ted where the men's room is, but when he finds it he can't get in. It has one of those combination locks on it that require him to push a number. The receptionist didn't tell him the number. He stands in the hall for a long time, feeling lost. He really needs to go to the bathroom, but for some reason he's scared to ask the receptionist for the combination. Finally, a man appears and, as Ted reads the fire-drill instructions, unlocks the door. Ted manages to grab it just before it shuts.

Diane is waiting in a bar for Ted. When they stopped having their affair, about a month ago, Ted agreed that he would still meet her, alone, once a week. They just talk. He thinks these meetings are unnecessary, but he always shows up. Ted lets Diane pick the place because he is afraid if he picks it they will see someone he knows. Since he started his aggressive search for employment, he is trying to straighten out his life. He is secretly looking forward to the fall: Diane will go back to college—all the way to Ohio; he will (hopefully) have a good new job; and his ex-wife will stop swimming in his pool.

Today Diane has picked a bar in the East Village that is known only by its address. It is five past five; Ted is five minutes late. Ted is usually fifteen or twenty minutes late. Once he was an hour late, and Diane waited the whole time, drinking drafts. When he finally arrived she went to the women's room and threw up. Then she drank some more with Ted.

This afternoon she is drinking a gin-and-tonic and watching MTV. There are two TVs over the door, and the duplication of the already bizarre images lends them a certain choreographed beauty. A man comes in and sits down across from her. It takes her a second to realize it is Ted.

"What happened?" she says. "You've shaved."

Ted rubs his naked cheek and shrugs. "How does it look?" he asks.

Ted looks younger; he looks like a boy. He looks like anything she said could hurt him. "Why did you shave?" Diane asks. "I thought you didn't care."

Ted shrugs again, and orders a Dos Equis.

Diane would like to touch his cheek but she restrains herself. She thinks about sitting on her hands but doesn't. They both look at the TV. On it, Michael Jackson dances down a deserted street, illuminating the squares of pavement with his every step. He scowls down at them, singing.

"Isn't he gorgeous?" asks Diane. "I think he's gorgeous."

Ted looks closely at Michael Jackson. He thinks Michael Jackson looks frightening, not gorgeous, but he doesn't tell Diane this. "When do you go back to school?" he says.

"After Labor Day," Diane says. "In two weeks."

"Are you looking forward to it?"

"I don't know," says Diane. "I suppose. Do you wish you were going back to school?"

"You mean to teaching?"

"Yes."

"No," says Ted. "I'm ready for something new."

"So am I," says Diane.

Ted's beer arrives and he pours it. It overflows. "Tell me something," he says.

"What?"

"Why didn't you get a real job this summer? In an office or something? Why did you babysit?"

Diane smiles. "There are no real jobs," she says. "You should know that. Besides, this is easy. He walks. He talks."

Ted nods.

"How did it go today?" Diane asks. "Did you get a job?"

"They don't tell you," says Ted. "There are second interviews. There are third interviews. They will get back to me."

"You're in a bad mood."

Ted doesn't answer.

"I try to transcend my bad moods," Diane says. "For the sake of others. Have you ever seen me in a bad mood?"

"No," says Ted.

"I've been in a bad mood all summer," says Diane. "I'm in a bad mood now." She smiles. "But can you tell? I still want to sleep with you. I want to touch your cheek more than anything in the world. But I'm transcending it. I'm sitting on my hands." She looks at her hands playing with the ice left in her glass. "Figuratively."

"Oh," says Ted.

"I think it's really sweet the way you humor me," Diane says. "Really, I do. I appreciate it."

Even though she sounds a little hysterical, Ted does not want Diane to stop talking. He doesn't know what to say to her. But Diane stops talking. She looks over at Ted.

"I've got to go," says Ted.

"You just got here," says Diane. "At least finish your beer."

Ted finishes his beer. He puts the glass down on the table and stands up. "I've got to go," he repeats. "I'm sorry."

"You're sorry?" Diane asks.

"Yes," Ted says.

"That's sweet, too," Diane says.

"If you want a snack before dinner, have one of these," Helen says, offering Mark one of the carrot sticks she is cutting.

"I'm not hungry," says Mark. "I don't want a snack."

"Oh," says Helen. "I thought you might be hungry."

"I'm not," says Mark.

"What did you have for lunch?" Helen asks. She likes talking to Mark alone. It is like a rehearsal for talking to Will when he grows up. It is good practice. Will Will be like Mark? Maybe. That wouldn't be bad. Mark is sweet. He gave her a card on Mother's Day that was a real Mother's Day card. Ted told Mark he could write in STEP before MOTHER, but Mark said no. She keeps the card in her bureau drawer. It has roses on it, and one of the roses has a plastic dewdrop on it.

"I had frozen pizza," Mark says. "But it was about three o'clock."

"What time did you get up?"

"I don't know," Mark says. "Eleven."

Helen is happy because Ted just called from the Port Authority to say he would be home for dinner. Will is sitting on the kitchen floor playing with the latches on her briefcase. In a few minutes he will want to be picked up. Mark is sitting at the kitchen table counting the money he's collected from his paper route. He is using the calculator she and Ted gave him for his birthday. It beeps, not unbeautifully, each time he pushes a button.

Annette left her sunglasses by the pool. At least she thinks she did. She can't find them anywhere in the house, and if Helen finds them by the pool her name will be shit. She'll know they're Annette's because they have her initials stuck to the corner of one of the lenses: AEV. What a dumb thing to have on my sunglasses, Annette thinks. I should have known better. She'll have to get Mark to hide them till tomorrow. Annette dials Ted's number but Helen answers. It figures. Annette hangs up, but then she realizes she has every right to talk to her son and Helen won't even think it's strange she's calling. She dials again. Once more Helen answers.

"Helen? This is Annette. We were just cut off." She shouldn't have said that. Now it is obvious that she hung up.

"Hi," says Helen. "How are you?"

"Fine," says Annette. "Is Mark there?"

"He's right here," says Helen.

"Hello, this is Mark speaking," Mark says, as he has been taught to say.

"Hello, Mark Speaking," says Annette. "This is Mommy Speaking. Listen. Just say yes or no, Mark. Don't repeat what I say."

"O.K.," says Mark.

"Yes or no," says Annette.

"Yes," says Mark.

"I think I left my sunglasses by the pool. I don't want to leave them there overnight. Did you find them?"

"No," says Mark.

"Do you see them? They would be on the picnic table. Or under the chair. The one I lie on."

"I can't see from here," says Mark.

"No," corrects Annette. "That was a no. Nada. Negative."

"What?" says Mark.

"Nothing. Honey, could you go outside and see if they're there? Not right now—wait a few minutes. If you see them just hide them someplace till tomorrow. O.K.?"

"O.K.," says Mark. "Yes."

"I love you, honey," Annette says. "I'll see you tomorrow."

"O.K.," says Mark. "Yes."

Helen and Mark and Ted are playing Spud in the backyard. Actually, since neither Helen nor Ted remembers exactly how to play, it's a variation of Spud: they take turns throwing the ball high up into the air, clapping first once, then twice, and so on, and then trying to catch the ball. Will is crawling around, getting in the way, his fat knees grass-stained. After a while it gets too dark to play

Spud so Ted and Mark start playing a violent game which mainly involves running around, screaming, and tackling each other. Helen takes Will inside for his bath. She fills the kitchen sink with warm soapy water, undresses Will, and slips his perfect body into the water. Will loves water. He spends the whole day in the pool, and now he sits in his bath, gurgling, patting the water ecstatically. Helen moves her suddenly large hands over and over Will, caressing as much as cleaning him, watching out the window as Ted and Mark roll together on the grass. This is all so perfect, she thinks. This is perfect.

Ted is lying on the couch reading one of Will's books. He is reading about a pig that builds a house. A busload of bunny rabbits moves into the house. They will be happy there. Will is sleeping and Helen is reading in bed. Mark is lying on the living-room floor, watching MTV. Ted sits on the couch, his bare feet resting lightly on Mark's back. "What did you do today?" he asks.

"Nothing," Mark says. "Played."

"What did you play?"

"Games," says Mark. He doesn't look up. He is looking at the TV. On it, people eat a huge banquet with their hands while a cat stalks down the middle of the table. Ted can't understand the words to the song. He starts to massage Mark's back with his feet.

"Does that feel good?" he asks.

"A little."

"Was Mommy here today?"

"Yes," says Mark.

"Isn't there a movie on?"

"I don't know," says Mark. "Probably."

"This is weird," says Ted. "Do you like this?"

"Not really," says Mark. "Their mouths aren't even right. Look."

Ted looks at the TV. The singer is a beat behind the music. He is obviously lip-synching to a pre-recorded soundtrack. "Tell me something," says Ted.

"What?"

"I don't know. Just something."

Mark turns his head away from the TV and rests his cheek on the floor, so he is looking at Ted. His eyes are closed. "Mommy left her sunglasses here," Mark says. "I found them. They're hidden in the laundry room."

"Oh," says Ted. "Are you tired?"

"A little."

"I am," says Ted. "I'm very tired."

"Go to bed, then," says Mark.

"I will," says Ted. "I'm going to. But not before you."

"I can put myself to bed," says Mark.

"Can you?"

"Yes."

Ted stands up and turns the TV off. The picture quickly shrinks and then disappears. Ted looks at the blank screen for a second, as if the picture might reappear. He cannot believe it was gotten rid of that easily. "Where in the laundry room?" he asks.

"What?" says Mark.

"Where did you hide Mommy's sunglasses? Where in the laundry room?"

Mark looks up at Ted. One of his cheeks is scarred from the carpeting. "It's a secret," he says.

On his way to the bedroom, Ted checks on Will. He stands by the crib and watches Will sleep. Is Will dreaming? When Ted was little, he had a dog that whimpered and shivered in her sleep, and Ted's mother always said it was because she was dreaming of chasing rabbits. Ted never knew what to make of this theory. The dog never chased rabbits when it was awake, so how could she dream about it? He watches Will sleep for a long time, half expecting him to whimper, or shiver.

Brushing his teeth, Ted wishes he had his beard back. He should have held out a little longer. That afternoon, he didn't know what to do with the hair that collected in his friend's sink. He was afraid to wash it down the drain, and he didn't want his friend to find it in the wastepaper basket. Finally, he wrapped it carefully in newspaper, took it out with him, and threw it surreptitiously into a garbage can, like something stolen or explosive. Ted can't understand why, given the fact he's seriously looking for a job, stopped seeing Diane, realized he truly loves Helen, why then doesn't he feel better about himself? He still must be doing something wrong. He looks in the mirror at his newly shaved face. He has trouble recognizing himself.

In the bedroom, Helen lowers her book and watches him undress. She smiles, leans forward. If Ted could only think of what it is he's doing wrong, he would change it, at once, so everything would be O.K. again. He wishes music would begin, so he could move his lips, and explain this, and everything else, to Helen.

Jason, my uncle's lover, sat in the dark kitchen eating what sounded like a bowl of cereal. He had some disease that made him hungry every few hours—something about not enough sugar in his blood. Every night, he got up at about three o'clock and fixed himself a snack. Since I was sleeping on the living-room couch, I could hear him.

My parents and I had driven down from Oregon to visit my Uncle Walter, who lived in Arizona. He was my father's younger brother. My sister Jackie got to stay home, on account of having just graduated from high school and having a job at the Lob-Steer Restaurant. But there was no way my parents were letting me stay home: I had just finished ninth grade and I was unemployed.

My parents slept in the guest room. Jason and Uncle Walter slept together in the master bedroom. The first morning, when I went into the bathroom, I saw Jason sitting on the edge of the big unmade bed in his jockey shorts. Jason was very tan, but it was an odd tan: his face and the bottom three-quarters of his arms were much darker than his chest. It looked as if he was wearing a T-shirt.

The living-room couch was made of leather and had little metal nubs stuck all over it. It was almost impossible to sleep on. I lay there listening to Jason crunch. The only other noise was the air-conditioner, which turned itself off and on constantly to maintain the same, ideal temperature. When it went off, you could hear the insects outside. A small square of light from the opened refrigerator appeared on the dining-room wall. Jason was putting the milk away. The faucet ran for a second, and then Jason walked through the living room, his white underwear bright against his body. I pretended I was asleep.

After a while, the air-conditioner went off, but I didn't hear the insects. At some point in the night—the point that seems closer to morning than to evening—they stopped their drone, as though they were unionized and paid to sing only so long. The house was very quiet. In the master bedroom, I could hear bodies moving, and murmuring, but I couldn't tell if it was people making love or turning over and over, trying to get comfortable. It went on for a few minutes, and then it stopped.

We were staying at Uncle Walter's for a week, and every hour of every day was planned. We always had a morning activity and an afternoon activity. Then we had cocktail hour, then dinner, then some card game. Usually hearts, with the teams switching: some nights Jason and Walter versus my parents, some nights the brothers challenging Jason and my mother. I never played. I watched TV, or rode Jason's moped around the deserted roads of Gretna Green, which was the name of Uncle Walter's condominium village. The houses in Gretna Green were called villas, and they all had different names—some for gems, some for colors, and some for animals. Uncle Walter and Jason lived in Villa Indigo.

We started each morning on the patio, where we'd eat breakfast and "plan the day." The adults took a long time planning the day so there would be less day to spend. All the other villa inhabitants ate breakfast on their patios, too. The patios were separated by lawn and rock gardens and pine trees, but there wasn't much privacy: everyone could see everyone else sitting under uniformly striped umbrellas, but everyone pretended he couldn't. They were mostly old people, retired people. Children were allowed only as guests. Everyone looked at me as if I was a freak.

Wednesday morning, Uncle Walter was inside making coffee in the new coffee machine my parents had brought him. My mother told me that whenever you're invited to someone's house overnight you should bring something —a hostess gift. Or a host gift, she added. She was helping Uncle Walter make breakfast. Jason was lying on a chaise in the sun, trying to even out his tan. My father was reading the *Wall Street Journal.* He got up early every morning and drove into town and bought it, so he could "stay in touch." My mother made him throw it away right after he read it so it wouldn't interfere with the rest of the day.

Jason had his eyes closed, but he was talking. He was listing the things we could do that day. I was sitting on the edge of a big planter filled with pachysandra and broken statuary that Leonard, my uncle's ex-boyfriend, had dug up somewhere. Leonard was an archeologist. He used to teach paleontology at Northern Arizona University, but he didn't get tenure, so he took a job with an oil company in South America, making sure the engineers didn't drill in sacred spots. The day before, I'd seen a tiny, purple-throated lizard in the vines, and I was trying to find him again. I wanted to catch him and take him back to Oregon.

Jason paused in his list, and my father said, "Uh-huh." That's what he always says when he's reading the newspaper and you talk to him.

"We could go to the dinosaur museum," Jason said.

"What's that?" I said.

Jason sat up and looked at me. That was the first thing I'd said to him, I think. I'd been ignoring him.

"Well, I've never been there," he said. Even though it was early in the morning, his brown forehead was already beaded with sweat. "It has some reconstructed dinosaurs and footprints and stuff."

"Let's go there," I said. "I like dinosaurs."

"Uh-huh," said my father.

My mother came through the sliding glass doors carrying a platter of scrambled eggs. Uncle Walter followed with the coffee.

"We're going to go to the dinosaur museum this morning," Jason said.

"Please, not that pit," Uncle Walter said.

"But Evan wants to go," Jason said. "It's about time we did something he liked."

Everyone looked at me. "It doesn't matter," I said.

"Oh, no," Uncle Walter said. "Actually, it's fascinating. It just brings back bad memories."

As it turned out, Uncle Walter and my father stayed home to discuss their finances. My grandmother had left them her money jointly, and they're always arguing about how to invest it. Jason drove my mother and me out to the dinosaur museum. I think my mother came just because she didn't want to leave me alone with Jason. She doesn't trust Uncle Walter's friends, but she doesn't let on. My father thinks it's very important we all treat Uncle Walter normally. Once he hit Jackie because she called Uncle Walter a fag. That's the only time he's ever hit either of us.

The dinosaur museum looked like an airplane hangar in the middle of the desert. Inside, trenches were dug into the earth and bones stuck out of their walls. They were still exhuming some of the skeletons. The sand felt oddly damp. My mother took off her sandals and carried them; Jason looked around quickly, and then went outside and sat on the hood of the car, smoking, with his shirt off. At the gift stand, I bought a small bag of dinosaur bone chips. My mother bought a 3-D panoramic postcard. When you held it one way, a dinosaur stood with a creature in its toothy mouth. When you tilted it, the creature disappeared. Swallowed.

On the way home, we stopped at a Safeway to do some grocery shopping. Both Jason and my mother seemed reluctant to push the shopping cart, so I did. In the produce aisle, Jason picked up cantaloupes and shook them next to his ear. A few feet away, my mother folded back the husks to get a good look at the kernels on the corncobs. It seemed as if everyone was pawing at the food. It made me nervous, because once, when I was little, I opened up a box of chocolate Ding Dongs in the grocery store and started eating one, and the manager came over and yelled at me. The only good thing about that was that my mother was forced to buy the Ding Dongs, but every time I ate one I felt sick.

A man in Bermuda shorts and a yellow cardigan sweater started talking to Jason. My mother returned with six apparently decent ears of corn. She dumped them into the cart. "Who's that?" she asked me, meaning the man Jason was talking to.

"I don't know," I said. The man made a practice golf swing, right there in the produce aisle. Jason watched him. Jason was a golf pro at a country club. He used to be part of the golf tour you see on television on weekend afternoons, but he quit. Now he gave lessons at the country club. Uncle Walter had been one of his pupils. That's how they met.

"It's hard to tell," Jason was saying. "I'd try opening up your stance a little more." He put a cantaloupe in our shopping cart.

"Hi," the man said to us.

"Mr. Baird, I'd like you to meet my wife, Ann," Jason said.

Mr. Baird shook my mother's hand. "How come we never see you down the club?"

"Oh . . ." my mother said.

"Ann hates golf," Jason said.

"And how 'bout you?" The man looked at me. "Do you like golf?"

"Sure," I said.

"Well, we'll have to get you out on the links. Can you beat your dad?"

"Not yet," I said.

"It won't be long," Mr. Baird said. He patted Jason on the shoulder. "Nice to see you, Jason. Nice to meet you, Mrs. Jerome."

He walked down the aisle and disappeared into the bakery section. My mother and I both looked at Jason. Even though it was cold in the produce aisle, he was sweating. No one said anything for a few seconds. Then my mother said, "Evan, why don't you go find some Doritos? And some Gatorade, too, if you want."

Back at Villa Indigo, my father and Uncle Walter were playing cribbage. Jason kissed Uncle Walter on the top of his semi-bald head. My father watched and then stood up and kissed my mother. I didn't kiss anyone.

Thursday, my mother and I went into Flagstaff to buy new school clothes. Back in Portland, when we go into malls we separate and make plans to meet at a specified time and place, but this was different: it was a strange mall, and since it was school clothes, my mother would pay for them, and therefore she could help pick them out. So we shopped together, which we hadn't done in a while. It was awkward. She pulled things off the rack which I had ignored, and when I started looking at the Right Now for Young Men stuff she entered the Traditional Shoppe. We finally bought some underwear, and some orange and yellow socks, which my mother said were "fun."

Then we went to the shoe store. I hate trying on shoes. I wish the salespeople would just give you the box and let you try them on yourself. There's something about some- one else doing it all—especially touching your feet—that embarrasses me. It's as if the person was your servant or something. And in this case the salesperson was a girl about my age, and I could tell she thought I was weird, shopping with my mother. My mother sat in the chair beside me, her pocketbook in her lap. She was wearing sneakers with little bunny-rabbit tails sticking out the back from her socks.

"Stand up," the girl said.

I stood up.

"How do they feel?" my mother asked.

"O.K.," I said.

"Walk around," my mother commanded.

I walked up the aisle, feeling everyone watching me. Then I walked back and sat down. I bent over and unlaced the shoes.

"So what do you think?" my mother asked.

The girl stood there, picking her nails. "They look very nice," she said.

I just wanted to get out of there. "I like them," I said. We bought the shoes.

On the way home, we pulled into a gas station–bar in the desert. "I can't face Villa Indigo without a drink," my mother said.

"What do you mean?" I asked.

"Nothing," she said. "Are you having a good time?"

"Now?"

"No. On this trip. At Uncle Walter's."

"I guess so," I said.

"Do you like Jason?"

"Better than Leonard."

"Leonard was strange," my mother said. "I never warmed to Leonard."

We got out of the car and walked into the bar. It was dark inside, and empty. A fat woman sat behind the bar, making something out of papier-mâché. It looked like one of those statues of the Virgin Mary people have in their front yards. "Hiya," she said. "What can I get you?"

My mother asked for a beer and I asked for some cranberry juice. They didn't have any, so I ordered a Coke. The woman got my mother's beer from a portable cooler like the ones you take to football games. It seemed very unprofessional. Then she sprayed Coke into a glass with one of those showerhead things. My mother and I sat at a table in the sun, but it wasn't hot, it was cold. Above us, the air-conditioner dripped.

My mother drank her beer from the long-necked green bottle. "What do you think your sister's doing right now?" she asked.

"What time is it?"

"Four."

"Probably getting ready to go to work. Taking a shower."

My mother nodded. "Maybe we'll call her tonight."

I laughed, because my mother called her every night. She would always make Jackie explain all the noises in the background. "It sounds like a party to me," she kept repeating.

My Coke was flat. It tasted weird, too. I watched the woman at the bar. She was poking at her statue with a swizzlestick—putting in eyes, I thought.

"How would you like to go see the Petrified Forest?" my mother asked.

"We're going to another national park?" On the way to Uncle Walter's, we had stopped at the Grand Canyon and taken a mule ride down to the river. Halfway down, my mother got hysterical, fell off her mule, and wouldn't get back on. A helicopter had to fly into the canyon and rescue her. It was horrible to see her like that.

"This one's perfectly flat," she said. "And no mules."

"When?" I said.

"We'd go down on Saturday and come back to Walter's on Monday. And leave for home Tuesday."

The bar woman brought us a second round of drinks. We had not asked for them. My Coke glass was still full. My mother drained her beer bottle and looked at the new one. "Oh dear," she said. "I guess we look like we need it."

The next night, at six-thirty, as my parents left for their special anniversary dinner in Flagstaff, the automatic lawn sprinklers went on. They were activated every evening. Jason explained that if the lawns were watered during the day the beads of moisture would magnify the sun's rays and burn the grass. My parents walked through the whirling water, got in their car, and drove away.

Jason and Uncle Walter were making dinner for me—steaks, on their new electric barbecue. I think they thought steak was a good, masculine food. Instead of charcoal, their grill had little lava rocks on the bottom. They reminded me of my dinosaur bone chips.

The steaks came in packs of two, so Uncle Walter was cooking up four. The fourth steak worried me. Who was it for? Would we split it? Was someone else coming to dinner?

"You're being awfully quiet," Uncle Walter said. For a minute, I hoped he was talking to the steaks—they weren't sizzling—so I didn't answer.

Then Uncle Walter looked over at me. "Cat got your tongue?" he asked.

"What cat?" I said.

"The cat," he said. "The proverbial cat. The big cat in the sky."

"No," I said.

"Then talk to me."

"I don't talk on demand," I said.

Uncle Walter smiled down at his steaks, lightly piercing them with his chef's fork. "Are you a freshman?" he asked.

"Well, a sophomore now," I said.

"How do you like being a sophomore?"

My lizard appeared from beneath a crimson leaf and clicked his eyes in all directions, checking out the evening.

"It's not something you like or dislike," I said. "It's something you are."

"Ah," Uncle Walter said. "So you're a fatalist?"

I didn't answer. I slowly reached out my hand toward the lizard, even though I was too far away to touch it. He clicked his eyes toward me but didn't move. I think he recognized me. My arm looked white and disembodied in the evening light.

Jason slid open the terrace doors, and the music from the stereo was suddenly loud. The lizard darted back under the foliage.

"I need a prep chef," Jason said. "Get in here, Evan."

I followed Jason into the kitchen. On the table was a wooden board, and on that was a tomato, an avocado, and an apple. Jason handed me a knife. "Chop those up," he said.

I picked up the avocado. "Should I peel this?" I asked. "Or what?"

Jason took the avocado and sliced it in half. One half held the pit and the other half held nothing. Then he pulled the warty skin off in two curved pieces and handed the naked globes back to me. "Now chop it."

I started chopping the stuff. Jason took three baked potatoes out of the oven. I could tell they were hot by the way he tossed them onto the counter. He made slits in them and forked the white stuffing into a bowl.

"What are you doing?" I asked.

"Making baked potatoes," he said. He sliced butter into the bowl.

"But why are you taking the potato out of the skin?"

"Because these are stuffed potatoes. You take the potato out and doctor it up and then put it back in. Do you like cheese?"

"Yes," I said.

"Do you like chives?"

"I don't know," I said. "I've never had them."

"You've never had chives?"

"My mother makes normal food," I said. "She leaves the potato in the skin."

"That figures," Jason said.

After dinner, we went to the driving range. Jason bought two large buckets and we followed him upstairs to the second level. I sat on a bench and watched Jason and my uncle hit ball after ball out into the floodlit night. Sometimes the balls arched up into the darkness, then reappeared as they fell.

Uncle Walter wasn't too good. A few times, he topped the ball and it dribbled over the edge and fell on the grass right below us. When that happened, he looked around to see who noticed, and winked at me.

"Do you want to hit some?" he asked me, offering his club.

"Sure," I said. I was on the golf team last fall, but this spring I played baseball. I think golf is an élitist sport. Baseball is more democratic.

I teed up a ball and took a practice swing, because my father, who taught me to play golf, told me always to take a practice swing. Always. My first shot was pretty good. It didn't go too far, but it went straight out and bounced a ways before I lost track of it in the shadows. I hit another.

Jason, who was in the next cubicle, put down his club

and watched me. "You have a great natural swing," he said.

His attention bothered me, and I almost missed my next ball. It rolled off the tee. I picked it up and re-teed it.

"Wait," Jason said. He walked over and stood behind me. "You're swinging much too hard." He leaned over me so that he was embracing me from behind, his large tan hands on top of mine, holding the club. "Now, just relax," he said, his voice right beside my cheek.

I tried to relax, but I couldn't. I suddenly felt very hot.

"O.K.," Jason said, "nice and easy. Keep the left arm straight." He raised his arms, and with them the club. Then we swung through, and he held the club still in the air, pointed out into the night. He let go of the club and ran his hand along my left arm, from my wrist up to my shoulder. "Straight," he said. "Keep it nice and straight." Then he stepped back and told me to try another swing by myself.

I did.

"Looking good," Jason said.

"Why don't you finish the bucket?" my uncle said. "I'm going down to get a beer."

Jason returned to his stall and resumed his practice. I teed up another ball, hit it, then another, and another, till I'd established a rhythm, whacking ball after ball, and all around me clubs were cutting the night, filling the sky with tiny white meteorites.

Back at Villa Indigo, the sprinklers had stopped, but the insects were making their strange noise in the trees. Jason and I went for a swim while my uncle watched TV. Jason wore a bathing suit like the swimmers in the Olympics: red-white-and-blue, and shaped like underwear. We walked out the terrace doors and across the wet lawn toward the pool, which was deserted and glowed bright blue. Jason dived in and swam some laps. I practiced diving off the board into the deep end, timing my dives so they wouldn't interfere with him. After about ten laps, he started treading water in the deep end and looked up at me. I was bouncing on the diving board.

"Want to play a game?" he said.

"What?"

Jason swam to the side and pulled himself out of the pool. "Jump or Dive," he said. "We'll play for money."

"How do you play?"

"Don't you know anything?" Jason said. "What do you do in Ohio?"

"It's Oregon," I said. "Not much."

"I can believe it. This is a very simple game. One person jumps off the diving board—jumps high—and when he's at the very highest the other person yells either 'Jump' or 'Dive,' and the person has to dive if the other person yells 'Dive' and jump if he yells 'Jump.' If you do the wrong thing, you owe the guy a quarter. O.K.?"

"O.K.," I said. "You go first."

I stepped off the diving board and Jason climbed on. "The higher you jump, the more time you have to twist," he said.

"Go," I said. "I'm ready."

Jason took three steps and sprang, and I yelled, "Dive." He did.

He got out of the pool, grinning. "O.K.," he said. "Your turn."

I sprang off the board and heard Jason yell, "Jump," but I was already falling forward head first. I tried to twist backward, but it was still a dive.

"You owe me a quarter," Jason said when I surfaced. He was standing on the diving board, bouncing. I swam to the side. "Here I go," he said.

I waited till he was coming straight down toward the water, feet first, before I yelled, "Dive," but somehow Jason somersaulted forward and dived into the pool.

We played for about fifteen minutes, until I owed Jason two dollars and twenty-five cents and my body was covered with red welts from smacking the water at bad angles. Suddenly the lights in the pool went off.

"It must be ten o'clock," Jason said. "Time for the geriatrics to go to bed."

The black water looked cold and scary. I got out and sat in a chair. We hadn't brought towels with us, and I shivered. Jason stayed in the pool.

"It's warmer in the water," he said.

I didn't say anything. With the lights off in the pool, the stars appeared brighter in the sky. I leaned my head back and looked up at them.

Something landed with a splat on the concrete beside me. It was Jason's bathing suit. I could hear him in the pool. He was swimming slowly underwater, coming up for a breath and then disappearing again. I knew that at some point he'd get out of the water and be naked, so I walked across the lawn toward Villa Indigo. Inside, I could see Uncle Walter lying on the couch, watching TV.

Later that night, I woke up hearing noises in the kitchen. I assumed it was Jason, but then I heard talking, and realized it was my parents, back from their anniversary dinner.

I got up off the couch and went into the kitchen. My mother was leaning against the counter, drinking a glass of seltzer. My father was sitting on one of the barstools, smoking a cigarette. He put it out when I came in. He's not supposed to smoke anymore. We made a deal in our family last year involving his quitting: my mother would lose fifteen pounds, my sister would take Science Honors (and pass), and I was supposed to brush Princess Leia, our dog, every day without having to be told.

"Our little baby," my mother said. "Did we wake you up?"

"Yes," I said.

"This is the first one I've had in months," my father said. "Honest. I just found it lying here."

"I told him he could smoke it," my mother said. "As a special anniversary treat."

"How was dinner?" I asked.

"O.K.," my mother said. "The restaurant didn't turn around, though. It was broken."

"That's funny," my father said. "I could have sworn it was revolving."

"You were just drunk," my mother said.

"Oh, no," my father said. "It was the stars in my eyes." He leaned forward and kissed my mother.

She finished her seltzer, rinsed the glass, and put it in the sink. "I'm going to bed," she said. "Good night."

My father and I both said good night, and my mother walked down the hall. My father picked up his cigarette. "It wasn't even very good," he said. He looked at it, then held it under his nose and smelled it. "I think it was stale. Just my luck."

I took the cigarette butt out of his hands and threw it away. When I turned around, he was standing by the terrace doors, looking out at the dark trees. It was windy.

"Have you made up your mind?" he asked.

"About what?"

"The trip."

"What trip?"

My father turned away from the terrace. "Didn't Mom tell you? Uncle Walter said you could stay here while Mom and I went down to see the Petrified Forest. If you want to. You can come with us otherwise."

"Oh," I said.

"I think Uncle Walter would like it if he had some time alone with you. I don't think he feels very close to you anymore. And he feels bad Jackie didn't come."

"Oh," I said. "I don't know."

"Is it because of Jason?"

"No," I said.

"Because I'd understand if it was."

"No," I said, "it's not that. I like Jason. I just don't know if I want to stay here. . . ."

"Well, it's no big deal. Just two days." My father reached up and turned off the light. It was a dual overhead light and fan, and the fan spun around some in the darkness, each spin slower. My father put his hands on my shoulders and half pushed, half guided me back to the couch. "It's late," he said. "See you tomorrow."

I lay on the couch. I couldn't fall asleep, because I knew that in a while Jason would be up for his snack. That kept me awake, and the decision about what to do. For some reason, it did seem like a big deal: going or staying. I could still picture my mother, backed up against the wall of the Grand Canyon, as far from the cliff as possible, crying, her mule braying, the helicopter whirring in the sky above us. It seemed like a choice between that and Jason swimming in the dark water, slowly and nakedly. I didn't want to be there for either.

The thing was, after I sprang off the diving board I did hear Jason shout, but my brain didn't make any sense of it. I could just feel myself hanging there, above the horrible bright-blue water, but I couldn't make my body turn, even though I was dropping dangerously, and much too fast.

Archeology

‹‹‹   ›››

Thursday

They are in McDonald's discussing their future. The man is eating an Egg McMuffin and drinking coffee; the woman is eating a cinnamon Danish and drinking a diet 7-Up. I think it would be best if I leave Tuesday after dinner, the man says. The woman says nothing. We'll have dinner together and then I'll leave, he says. The woman gets up and orders another diet 7-Up. A young man takes her order, circling the proper items on his pad. He has curly blond hair, he calls her Ma'am, and she can tell by watching his hands that he is a virgin. His hands are small and white—they almost look like a woman's—and she can tell they have never touched another person, really touched, intimately touched. The woman is fascinated by hands. Her father left her mother for a pianist when she was ten. She hated her father and she hated the pianist—the pianist's name was Victoria—until she was seventeen and saw a picture of the pianist for the first time. The pianist was standing in front of a fireplace, and her arm rested along the mantelpiece and her hand dropped over the edge and was silhouetted against the fire. It was just one of her hands—the other one wasn't in the picture, or if it was she can't remember where in the picture it was—but it was the most beautiful hand she had ever seen, and looking at it—the incredibly long, slender fingers framed in the firelight—she understood why her father loved the pianist, why he had left her mother; and the more she looked at the picture the more she began to love the pianist, too. Her hands are very small and it doesn't bother her except when she and the man—the one who is going to leave her Tuesday after dinner, who's eating an Egg McMuffin now—are making love. When they make love she's aware of how small her hands are against his back or stroking his thighs. She wishes, when they make love, that she had hands like the pianist so she could touch more of the man all at once. The boy gives her the diet 7-Up and her hand touches his hand on the paper cup—his beneath hers, hers touching his— but quickly he pulls his hand away, spilling a little of the diet 7-Up on the silver counter, where it beads like mercury, and she walks to the little table where the man is still sitting, even though he is planning to leave her.

Friday

On her way home from work she stops at the library. She is supposed to stop at the liquor store and buy wine for a special dinner the man is making—the man is home now, making the special dinner—but since he announced his intention to leave her Tuesday after dinner she has become indifferent to his requests. Let him get his own wine. Besides, at the liquor store you have to pay for things and she dreads paying for things. When the man leaves—Tuesday, after dinner—she will have to do all her shopping herself. This is one of the worst points concerning his leaving. There are many bad points, but that is the one she is most concerned with now. Perhaps she will starve when the man leaves. In college she almost starved because she was unable to eat in public, in the cafeteria. She hates eating in public—something about the way her mouth moves, and the color of the food against her lips and all the people watching. When she weighed eighty-five pounds—about a third of the way through the first semester—her mother let her drop out. She gained the weight back quickly once she was allowed to eat alone, at home. When she gets in the library she has no idea why she came, what she's looking for. She rarely reads—maybe a magazine—but she hasn't read a book since she dropped out of college two years ago. She begins, very methodically, to look at every book in the library, touching its spine and whispering its title under her breath. When she's done with the first case she sees a book at the checkout counter propped up on a little stand. The book is called *Where We Came From: Archeology Explains* and on the cover is a picture of a man in a white safari suit holding a dirty skull and smiling. Next to the book is a little sign —one of the librarians probably wrote it—that says TAKE ME HOME. The librarian sees her looking at the book and says, May I help you? She is unsure what to say. She would like to take the book about archeology home but she might not have her library card or it might have expired or maybe this book about archeology is on reserve for someone special—maybe there's an archeology club in town she knows nothing about and the book is for them. But the sign says TAKE ME HOME so it must be O.K., so she asks the librarian if she can take the book about archeology out, and the librarian says yes but it's a two-week book, and she hands the librarian her card—it was in her wallet where she hoped it would be and it hasn't expired yet—and the librarian puts it in the machine and something happens to both of them, she really can't tell what—it happens so quickly—and the librarian gives her the book and then gives her back her card and says, Enjoy! Enjoy! and she goes outside with the book and it's dark and when she gets home the man will ask her where the wine is and she'll lie and say the liquor store is closed because the owner just died, and by the time the man finds out that she's lying he will have left her.

Saturday

They are in a bar and he is holding her up, high above the crowd, and she is swaying in the dark because the man is swaying beneath her, holding her, his mouth pressed tight against her; and below her, by the pool table, three men are having a fight and one of them picks up a pool ball— it's the purple one—and holds it high above his head threatening to throw it at the other men and the jukebox is playing very loudly—so loudly she can't even hear the men who are fighting swear at one another—the song Blondie sings that goes *I'm not the kind of girl* and the man, who's very drunk, is lowering her, slowly, still kissing her, his mouth wet with beer and his tongue pushing back toward her throat, and the man holding the pool ball high above his head—people are dancing around him—slams the pool ball toward the table but instead of smashing it into the table he drops it into the corner pocket and then looks sheepishly at his empty hand and she can tell the fight is over and the song on the jukebox—the one Blondie sings—is getting louder because it's getting closer to the end and the man's tongue is sliding out of her mouth and she's anticipating the way the floor will feel when her feet finally touch it, which they will, any second now.

Tuesday

Driving home, she thinks: Why go home to have dinner with the man when he's just going to leave after? She tries to think of a good reason to have dinner with the man, but she can't. She goes to the library to return the book on archeology. It has never left her car, and she knows now that she will never read it, she has lost interest in the little pictures of bones and pots and houses, dug up, carefully, from the earth. She goes into the library and slides the book in the return slot and waits to hear it fall onto the pile of books in the box. It falls quickly and makes a quiet thumping noise. The librarian looks at her and smiles. This is a different librarian but the smile is identical. She leaves the library and gets in the car and as soon as she pulls out into the traffic—it's getting dark by this time, the streetlights are on and she turns her lights on— as soon as she's driving in the traffic she realizes she misses the book about archeology, wishes she hadn't returned it so quickly. She slows down and considers turning around and getting it back again but she's not sure how to do it: the book is in the return box, probably still on the top, but it's not on the shelf or in the little stand that says TAKE ME HOME and she supposes she could ask the librarian—the one who smiled at her tonight—for surely she could reach down into the box and get the book about archeology back for her. A car honks. She's driving too slow so she speeds up and forgets about the book. She looks outside. The snow is finally melting, around the trees are great wet pools of grass as if the trees are sucking up the snow to prepare for spring, and watching the trees

reminds her—she's not sure why, maybe the smell because she's opened her window a little—of her last job,
the job she had before the job she has now. It was in a
slaughterhouse outside of Kansas City. Her job was to
write down the numbers tattooed on the cattle as they
filed past her into the slaughterhouse. A man, whose
name was Lesje, stood in the little pen the cattle filed
through and shouted out each number, and she had to
write it down on a little clipboard they gave her. They
were supposed to do two hundred an hour but usually
they did only about one hundred. One hour they did one
hundred eighty, but that was baby cows for veal and they
went much quicker. After a few days she found out she
was the last woman the cattle saw—after her it was all
men on the line—and she felt bad about that, as if being
the last woman they saw she ought to make a good last
impression on them. She started to reach out and touch
each one—just pat it a little on the shoulder—and she also
tried to look each one in the eye, but the cattle were scared
and shifty-eyed and it was hard to make contact with
them. For some reason she wanted to reassure them so
she'd reach out and touch them but it slowed her down
and she started to write the wrong numbers sometimes—
not that it mattered, no one ever looked at the long list of
numbers she compiled every day—and once she almost
got her hand caught in the gate that crashed down to
separate each cow from the next one. So she stopped
trying to touch them and a few days later she quit. She
drives into the parking lot and gets out of the car. When
she looks up at the apartment windows, they're dark and
she's glad because that means the man has gone—he's
really left—his car is gone, too, and she stands looking up
at the dark windows for a long time because she doesn't

want to go into the apartment now that the man is gone
and she doesn't want to get back in the car and go anywhere—the library is closed now anyway and she'll never
be able to get the book about archeology back—so she
just stands there, looking up at the windows, not thinking
anything really, but feeling the way she used to feel when
she was little and would turn a rock over to find something underneath it only to find nothing: just the cool,
hard curve of the rock and the brown earth, hollowed out,
nothing, not that she knew what she wanted to find, but
there was nothing there and she stands in the parking lot
feeling like that for a long time.

Excerpts from
Swan Lake

What is that called again?" my grandmother asks, nodding at my lover's wok.

"A wok," I say.

"A wok," my grandmother repeats. The word sounds strange coming out of her mouth. I can't remember ever hearing her say a foreign word. She is sitting at the kitchen table smoking a Players cigarette. She saw an ad for them in *Time* magazine and wanted to try them, so after work I drove her down to the 7-Eleven and she bought a pack. She also bought a Hostess cherry pie. That was for me.

Neal, my lover, is stir-frying mushrooms in the wok. My grandmother thinks he is my friend. I am slicing tomatoes and apples. We are staying at my grandmother's house while my parents go on a cruise around the world. It is a romance cruise, stopping at the "love capitals" of the world. My mother won it. Neal and I are making mushroom curry. Neal isn't wearing a shirt, and his chest is sweating. He always sweats when he cooks. He cooks with a passion.

"I wish I could help," my grandmother says. "Let me know if I can."

"We will," says Neal.

"I don't think I've seen a wok before," my grandmother says.

"Everyone has them now," says Neal. "They're great."

The doorbell rings, the front door opens, and someone shouts, "Yoo-hoo!"

"Who's that?" I say.

"Who's what?" my grandmother says. She's a little deaf.

I walk into the living room to investigate. A woman in a jogging suit is standing in the front hall. "Who are you?" she says.

"Paul," I say.

"Where's Mrs. Andrews?" she asks.

"In the kitchen," I say. "I'm her grandson."

"Oh," she says. "I thought you were some kind of maniac. What with that knife and all." She nods at my hand. I am still holding the knife.

"Who are you?" I ask.

"Who's there?" my grandmother shouts from the kitchen.

The woman shouts her name to my grandmother. It sounds like Gloria Marsupial. Then she whispers to me, "I'm from Meals on Wheels. I bring Mrs. Andrews dinner on Tuesday nights. Your mother bowls on Tuesday."

"Oh," I say.

Mrs. Marsupial walks past me into the kitchen. I follow her. "There you are," she says to my grandmother. "I thought he had killed you."

"Nonsense," my grandmother says. "What are you

doing here? You come on Tuesdays."

"It is Tuesday," says Mrs. Marsupial. She opens the oven. "We've got to warm this up."

"I don't need it tonight," my grandmother says. "They're making me dinner."

Mrs. Marsupial eyes the wok, the mushrooms, and Neal disdainfully.

"What do you have?" Neal asks.

Mrs. Marsupial takes a tinfoil tray out of the paper bag she is holding. It has a cardboard cover on it. "Meat loaf," she says. "And green beans. And a nice pudding."

"What kind of pudding?" my grandmother asks.

"Rice pudding," says Mrs. Marsupial.

"No thanks," says my grandmother.

"What are you making?" Mrs. Marsupial asks Neal.

"Mushroom curry," says Neal. "We're lacto-vegetarians."

"I'm sure you are," Mrs. Marsupial replies. She turns to my grandmother. "Well, do you want this or not?"

"I can have it tomorrow night," my grandmother says. "If I remember."

"Then I'll stick it in the fridge." Mrs. Marsupial opens the refrigerator and frowns at the beer Neal and I have installed. She moves a six-pack of Dos Equis aside to make room for the container. "I'll put it right here," she says into the refrigerator, "and tomorrow night you just pop it into the oven at about three hundred and warm it up, and it will be as good as new." She closes the refrigerator and looks at my grandmother. "Are you sure you're all right now?" she asks.

"What kind of bush is that out there?" my grandmother says. She points out the window.

"That's not a bush, dear," Mrs. Marsupial says. "That's the clothesline."

"I know that's the clothesline," my grandmother says. "I mean behind it. With the white flowers."

"It's a lilac bush," I say.

"A lilac? Are you sure?"

"It's a lilac," confirms Neal. "You can smell it when you hang out the wash." He opens the window and sticks his head out. "You can smell it from here," he says. "It's beautiful."

"Do you want me to take your blood pressure?" Mrs. Marsupial asks my grandmother. "I left the sphygmomanometer in the van."

"No," my grandmother says. "My blood pressure is fine. It's my memory that's no good."

I dump the sliced tomatoes and apples into the wok and lower the domelike cover. Then I stick my head out the window beside Neal's. It's getting dark. The lilac bush, the clothesline, the collapsing grape arbor are all disappearing.

"I don't want to be late for my next drop-off," Mrs. Marsupial says. "I guess I'll be running along."

No one says anything. Neal has taken my hand; we are holding hands outside the kitchen window where my grandmother and Mrs. Marsupial can't see us. The smell of curry mixes with the scent of lilacs and intoxicates me. I feel as if I'm leaning on the balcony of a Mediterranean villa, not the window of my grandmother's house in Cheshire, Connecticut, five feet above the dripping spigot.

After dinner my grandmother tells Neal and me stories about "growing up on the farm." She didn't really grow

up on a farm—she just visited a friend's farm one summer
—but these memories are particularly vivid and make for
good telling. I have heard them many times, but Neal
hasn't. He is lying on the floor at my feet, exhausted from
cooking. My grandmother is sitting on the love seat and
I am sitting across from her on the couch, stroking Neal's
bare back with my bare foot, a gesture that is hidden by
the coffee table. At least I think it is.

"There was an outhouse with a long bench and three
holes—a little one, a medium one, and a big one."

"Like the three bears," says Neal. His eyes are closed.

"Like who?" says my grandmother. She doesn't like
being interrupted.

"The three bears," repeats Neal. "Cinderella and the
three bears."

"Goldilocks," I correct.

"Little Red Riding Hood," murmurs Neal.

"You've lost me," my grandmother says. "Anyway, we
used to eat outside, on a big plank table under a big tree.
Was it an oak tree? No, it was a mulberry tree. I remember
because mulberries would fall off it if the wind blew.
You'd be eating mashed potatoes and suddenly there
would be a mulberry in them. They looked like black
raspberries. In between courses we would run down to the
barn and back—down the hill to the barn, touch it, and
run back up the hill. You'd always be hungry again when
you got back up." She pauses. "We should turn on some
light," she says. "We shouldn't sit in the dark."

No one says anything. No one turns on a light, because
light damages the way that words travel. Suddenly my
grandmother says, "How many times was I married?"

"Once," I say. "Just once."

"Are you sure just once?"

"As far as I know."

"Maybe you had affairs," suggests Neal.

"Oh, I'm sure I had affairs," says my grandmother. "Although I couldn't tell you with whom. I can't remember the faces at all. It all gets fuzzy. Sometimes I'm not even sure who you are."

"I'm Paul," I say. "Your beloved grandson."

"I'm Neal," Neal says. "Paul's friend."

"I know," my grandmother says. "I know now. But I'll wake up tonight and I'll have no idea. I won't even know where I am. Or what year it is."

"But none of that matters," I say.

"What?" my grandmother asks.

"Who cares what year it is?" I say. I rest both my feet lightly on Neal's back. It moves as though he is sleeping. I think about explaining how none of that matters: names or ages or whereabouts. But, before I can explain this to my grandmother, or attempt to, a new thought occurs to me: Someday, I'll forget Neal, just like my grandmother has forgotten the great love of her life. And then I think: Is Neal the great love of my life? Or is that one still coming, to be forgotten, too?

After my grandmother goes to bed at nine o'clock, Neal and I redo the dishes. She likes to wash them if we make the dinner, but she doesn't do such a hot job anymore. There are always little pieces of muck stuck to her pink glass plates. Neal washes and I dry. I am using a dish towel from the 1964 World's Fair. On it, a geisha girl embraces an Eskimo, who in turn embraces an Indian squaw embracing a man in a kilt. My grandmother took my sister and me to the World's Fair, but I don't remember her buying this dish towel.

"I think I'm going to move back into the apartment," Neal says.

"Why?" I ask.

"I feel funny here. I don't feel comfortable."

"But I thought you wanted to get out of the city in the summer?"

"I did. I do. But this isn't working out." Neal motions with his wet, sudsy hand, indicating my grandmother's kitchen: the African violets on the window sill, the humming refrigerator, the cookie jars filled with Social Teas. I insert the plate I am drying into the slotted dish rack. It seems to stand on its own accord, gleaming.

"Are you mad?" asks Neal.

"I don't know," I say. "Sad. But not mad."

"There is another thing, too," Neal says. He chases the suds down the drain with the sprayer thing.

"What?"

"I feel like when we're sleeping together she might come in. I don't feel right about it."

"She sleeps all night," I say. "She thinks you sleep on the porch. Plus she's senile."

"I know," says Neal, "but I still don't feel right about it. I just can't relax."

I sit down at the kitchen table and light one of my grandmother's Players cigarettes. Neal washes his hands, dries them, and carefully folds the World's Fair dish towel. He comes over and curls his fingers around my throat, lightly, affectionately throttling me. Neal's clean hands smell like the English Lavender soap my grandmother keeps in a pump dispenser by the sink. Neal's hands smell like my grandmother's hands.

I exhale and look at our reflection in the window. I only smoke about one cigarette a month, and every time I do

I experience a wonderful dizzy feeling that quickly gives way to nausea.

"It's no big deal," Neal says. "It's just not cool here."

I think about answering, but I can't. I close my eyes and feel myself floating. The occasional cigarette is a wonderful thing.

My mother sends me a postcard from Piraeus. This is what it says:

Dear Paul,

Piraeus is a lovely city considering I had never even heard of it. I'm not sure why it's a Love Capital except the movie "Never on Sunday" was filmed here. Have you seen it? Hope you're O.K. Are you taking good care of Grandma?

Love,
Mom

About a week after Neal moves out, the ballet comes to town, and my grandmother asks to see it. There are commercials for it on TV, showing an excerpt from *Swan Lake*, while across the bottom of the screen a phone number for charging tickets appears and disappears. The swan's feet blur into the flashing numbers.

My grandmother claims she has never been to the ballet. I don't know if I should believe her or not. Whenever the commercial comes on, she turns it up loud and calls for me to come watch. I do not understand her sudden zeal for the ballet. She gave up on movies long ago, because they were "just nonsense." Besides, she falls asleep at nine o'clock, no matter where she is.

Nevertheless, I buy three tickets to *Swan Lake* for my

grandmother's eighty-eighth birthday. Neal comes to her special birthday dinner, bringing a Carvel ice-cream cake with him. At my grandmother's request, we are eating tomatoes stuffed with tuna salad. She must have seen an ad for it somewhere. I tried to scallop the edges of the tomatoes as she described, but I failed: they looked hacked-at, like something that would be served in a punk restaurant. But they taste O.K.

"It's just like old times, having Neal here," my grandmother says.

"I've only been gone a week," Neal says.

"It seems like longer," my grandmother says. "It seems like ages. We were lonely without you. Weren't we, Paul?"

I don't answer. I never admit to being lonely.

After dinner Neal and I do the dishes because my grandmother is the birthday girl and not allowed to help. Neal is telling her the story of *Swan Lake.* "The chief swan turns into a girl and falls in love with the prince, but then she gets turned back into a swan."

"Why?" my grandmother asks.

"I don't know," Neal says. "It's morning or something. They have to part. But the prince goes back to the lake the next night and finds her, and because they truly love one another, she changes back into a girl. I think that's it. Basically."

"It sounds ridiculous," says my grandmother.

"I thought you especially wanted to see *Swan Lake,*" I say.

"I do," my grandmother says. "It just sounds silly." She looks out the window. "What kind of bush is that out there?" She points to the lilac bush.

"A lilac," I say.

"That's a lilac?" she says. "I thought lilacs had tiny purple flowers."

"They do," I say. "But that's a white lilac. The flowers grow in bunches."

"That's not a lilac," my grandmother says. "I remember lilacs."

"It is a lilac," says Neal. "Maybe you're thinking of wisteria. Or dogwood."

"I can't see it from here," my grandmother says. "I'm going to go out and look at it." She gets up and walks down the hall. The back door opens and then slams shut.

"If she asks me that one more time," I say, "I think I'll go crazy."

"I think it's sweet," Neal says. "I think your grandmother's great."

"I know," I say. "She is."

Neal puts the remaining, melting Carvel cake back into the freezer, and then stands there, with the freezer door open, pinching the pink sugar roses with his fingers. "I wish your grandmother knew we were lovers," he says.

I laugh. "I don't think she'd want to know that," I say. I sit down at the kitchen table.

"Why do you say that?" Neal says. "I think you should tell her. I wouldn't be surprised if she had figured it out."

"What do you mean?" I say.

"What do you mean, what do I mean?" Neal says.

"She doesn't know," I say. "No one knows."

"I know no one knows." Neal closes the freezer and sits down next to me. "That's the problem."

I look out the window. My grandmother is walking slowly down the backyard. She is an old lady, and I love her, and I love Neal, too, but I don't see the problem in all this. "I don't see the problem in all this," I say.

"You don't?" Neal says. "Really, you don't?"

I shake my head no. Neal shrugs and gets up. He opens the refrigerator and stands silhouetted in the glow from the open door. He is looking for nothing in particular. Outside, my grandmother reaches up and pulls a lilac blossom toward her face, because she has forgotten what they are.

Neal is disgusted with me, and leaves the ballet at intermission. My grandmother falls asleep as Prince Siegfried is reunited with Odette. Her hands are crossed in her lap. She is wearing a pair of white mismatched gloves—one has tiny pearls sewn on the back of the hand, and the other doesn't.

I watch the dancing, unamused. The ballet is such a lie. No one—not my grandmother, not Neal, not I—no one in real life ever moves that beautifully.

My dog, Keds, was sitting outside of the A & P last Thursday when he got smashed by some kid pushing a shopping cart. At first we thought he just had a broken leg, but later we found out he was bleeding inside. Every time he opened his mouth, blood would seep out like dull red words in a bad silent dream.

Every night before my sister goes to her job she washes her hair in the kitchen sink with beer and mayonnaise and eggs. Sometimes I sit at the table and watch the mixture dribble down her white back. She boils a pot of water on the stove at the same time; when she is finished with her hair, she steams her face. She wants so badly to be beautiful.

I am trying to solve complicated algebraic problems I have set for myself. Since I started cutting school last Friday, the one thing I miss is homework. Find the value for n. Will it be a whole number? It is never a whole number. It is always a fraction.

"Will you get me a towel?" my sister asks. She turns her face toward me and clutches her hair to the top of her head. The sprayer hose slithers into its hole next to the faucet.

I hand her a dish towel. "No," she says. "A bath towel. Don't be stupid."

In the bathroom, my mother is watering her plants. She has arranged them in the tub and turned the shower on. She sits on the toilet lid and watches. It smells like outdoors in the bathroom.

I hand my sister the towel and watch her wrap it around her head. She takes the cover off the pot of boiling water and drops lemon slices in. Then she lowers her face into the steam.

This is the problem I have set for myself:

$$\frac{245(n + 17)}{34} = 396(n - 45)$$

$$n =$$

Wednesday, I stand outside the high-school gym doors. Inside students are lined up doing calisthenics. It's snowing, and prematurely dark, and I can watch without being seen.

"Well," my father says when I get home. He is standing in the garage testing the automatic door. Every time a plane flies overhead, the door opens or closes, so my father is trying to fix it. "Have you changed your mind about school?" he asks me.

I lock my bicycle to a pole. This infuriates my father, who doesn't believe in locking things up in his own house. He pretends not to notice. I wipe the thin stripes of snow off the fenders with my middle finger. It is hard to ride a bike in the snow. This afternoon on my way home from the high school I fell off, and lay in the snowy road with my bike on top of me. It felt warm.

"We're going to get another dog," my father says.

"It's not that," I say. I wish everyone would stop talking about dogs. I can't tell how sad I really am about Keds versus how sad I am in general. If I don't keep these things separate, I feel as if I'm betraying Keds.

"Then what is it?" my father says.

"It's nothing," I say.

My father nods. He is very good about bringing things up and then letting them drop. A lot gets dropped. He presses the button on the automatic control. The door slides down its oiled tracks and falls shut. It's dark in the garage. My father presses the button again and the door opens, and we both look outside at the snow falling in the driveway, as if in those few seconds the world might have changed.

My mother has forgotten to call me for dinner, and when I confront her with this she tells me that she did but that I was sleeping. She is loading the dishwasher. My sister is standing at the counter, listening, and separating eggs for her shampoo.

"What can I get you?" my mother asks. "Would you like a meat-loaf sandwich?"

"No," I say. I open the refrigerator and survey its illuminated contents. "Could I have some eggs?"

"O.K.," my mother says. She comes and stands beside me and puts her hand on top of mine on the door handle. There are no eggs in the refrigerator. "Oh," my mother says; then, "Julie?"

"What?" my sister asks.

"Did you take the last eggs?"

"I guess so," my sister says. "I don't know."

"Forget it," I say. "I won't have eggs."

"No," my mother says. "Julie doesn't need them in her shampoo. That's not what I bought them for."

"I do," my sister says. "It's a formula. It doesn't work without the eggs. I need the protein."

"I don't want eggs," I say. "I don't want anything." I go into my bedroom.

My mother comes in and stands looking out the window. The snow has turned to rain. "You're not the only one who is unhappy about this," she says.

"About what?" I say. I am sitting on my unmade bed. If I pick up my room, my mother will make my bed: that's the deal. I didn't pick up my room this morning.

"About Keds," she says. "I'm unhappy, too. But it doesn't stop me from going to school."

"You don't go to school," I say.

"You know what I mean," my mother says. She turns around and looks at my room, and begins to pick things off the floor.

"Don't do that," I say. "Stop."

My mother drops the dirty clothes in an exaggerated gesture of defeat. She almost—almost—throws them on the floor. The way she holds her hands accentuates their emptiness. "If you're not going to go to school," she says, "the least you can do is clean your room."

In algebra word problems, a boat sails down a river while a jeep drives along the bank. Which will reach the capital first? If a plane flies at a certain speed from Boulder to Oklahoma City and then at a different speed from Oklahoma City to Detroit, how many cups of coffee can the stewardess serve, assuming she is unable to serve during the first and last ten minutes of each flight? How many times can a man ride the elevator to the top of the Empire State Building while his wife climbs the stairs, given that the woman travels one stair slower each flight? And if the man jumps up while the elevator is going down, which is moving—the man, the woman, the elevator, or the snow falling outside?

The next Monday I get up and make preparations for going to school. I can tell at the breakfast table that my mother is afraid to acknowledge them for fear it won't be true. I haven't gotten up before ten o'clock in a week. My mother makes me French toast. I sit at the table and write the note excusing me for my absence. I am eighteen, an adult, and thus able to excuse myself from school. This is what my note says:

> Dear Mr. Kelly [my homeroom teacher]:
> Please excuse my absence February 17–24. I was unhappy and did not feel able to attend school.
> Sincerely,
> MICHAEL PECHETTI

This is the exact format my mother used when she wrote my notes, only she always said, "Michael was home with a sore throat," or "Michael was home with a bad cold." The colds that prevented me from going to school were always bad colds.

My mother watches me write the note but doesn't ask to see it. I leave it on the kitchen table when I go to the bathroom, and when I come back to get it I know she has read it. She is washing the bowl she dipped the French toast into. Before, she would let Keds lick it clean. He liked eggs.

* * *

In Spanish class we are seeing a film on flamenco dancers. The screen wouldn't pull down, so it is being projected on the blackboard, which is green and cloudy with erased chalk. It looks a little like the women are sick, and dancing in Heaven. Suddenly the little phone on the wall buzzes.

Mrs. Smitts, the teacher, gets up to answer it, and then walks over to me. She puts her hand on my shoulder and leans her face close to mine. It is dark in the room. "Miguel," Mrs. Smitts whispers, *"tienes que ir a la oficina de* guidance."

"What?" I say.

She leans closer, and her hair blocks the dancers. Despite the clicking castanets and the roomful of students, there is something intimate about this moment. *"Tienes que ir a la oficina de* guidance," she repeats slowly. Then, "You must go to the guidance office. Now. *Vaya."*

My guidance counselor, Mrs. Dietrich, used to be a history teacher, but she couldn't take it anymore, so she was moved into guidance. On her immaculate desk is a calendar blotter with "LUNCH" written across the middle of every box, including Saturday and Sunday. The only other things on her desk are an empty photo cube and my letter to Mr. Kelly. I sit down, and she shows me the letter as if I haven't yet read it. I reread it.

"Did you write this?" she asks.

I nod affirmatively. I can tell Mrs. Dietrich is especially nervous about this interview. Our meetings are always charged with tension. At the last one, when I was selecting my second-semester courses, she started to laugh hysterically when I said I wanted to take Boys' Home Ec. Now every time I see her in the halls she stops me and asks how I'm doing in Boys' Home Ec. It's the only course of mine she remembers.

I hand the note back to her and say, "I wrote it this morning," as if this clarifies things.

"This morning?"

"At breakfast," I say.

"Do you think this is an acceptable excuse?" Mrs. Dietrich asks. "For missing more than a week of school?"

"I'm sure it isn't," I say.

"Then why did you write it?"

Because it is the truth, I start to say. It is. But somehow I know that saying this will make me more unhappy. It might make me cry. "I've been doing homework," I say.

"That's fine," Mrs. Dietrich says, "but it's not the point. The point is, to graduate you have to attend school for a hundred and eighty days, or have legitimate excuses for the days you've missed. That's the point. Do you want to graduate?"

"Yes," I say.

"Of course you do," Mrs. Dietrich says.

She crumples my note and tries to throw it into the wastepaper basket but misses. We both look for a second at the note lying on the floor, and then I get up and throw it away. The only other thing in her wastepaper basket is a banana peel. I can picture her eating a banana in her tiny office. This, too, makes me sad.

"Sit down," Mrs. Dietrich says.

I sit down.

"I understand your dog died. Do you want to talk about that?"

"No," I say.

"Is that what you're so unhappy about?" she says. "Or is it something else?"

I almost mention the banana peel in her wastebasket, but I don't. "No," I say. "It's just my dog."

Mrs. Dietrich thinks for a moment. I can tell she is embarrassed to be talking about a dead dog. She would be more comfortable if it were a parent or a sibling.

"I don't want to talk about it," I repeat.

She opens her desk drawer and takes out a pad of hall passes. She begins to write one out for me. She has beautiful handwriting. I think of her learning to write beautifully as a child and then growing up to be a guidance counselor, and this makes me unhappy.

"Mr. Neuman is willing to overlook this matter," she says. Mr. Neuman is the principal. "Of course, you will have to make up all the work you've missed. Can you do that?"

"Yes," I say.

Mrs. Dietrich tears the pass from the pad and hands it to me. Our hands touch. "You'll get over this," she says. "Believe me, you will."

My sister works until midnight at the Photo-Matica. It's a tiny booth in the middle of the A & P parking lot. People drive up and leave their film and come back the next day for the pictures. My sister wears a uniform that makes her look like a counterperson in a fast-food restaurant. Sometimes at night when I'm sick of being at home I walk downtown and sit in the booth with her.

There's a machine in the booth that looks like a printing press, only snapshots ride down a conveyor belt and fall into a bin and then disappear. The machine gives the illusion that your photographs are being developed on the spot. It's a fake. The same fifty photographs roll through over and over, and my sister says nobody notices, because everyone in town is taking the same pictures. She opens up the envelopes and looks at them.

Before I go into the booth, I buy cigarettes in the A & P. It is open twenty-four hours a day, and I love it late at night. It is big and bright and empty. The checkout girl sits on her counter swinging her legs. The Muzak plays "If Ever I Would Leave You." Before I buy the cigarettes, I walk up and down the aisles. Everything looks good to eat, and the things that aren't edible look good in their own way. The detergent aisle is colorful and clean-smelling.

My sister is listening to the radio and polishing her nails when I get to the booth. It is almost time to close.

"I hear you went to school today," she says.

"Yeah."

"How was it?" she asks. She looks at her fingernails, which are so long it's frightening.

"It was O.K.," I say. "We made chili dogs in Home Ec."

"So are you over it all?"

I look at the pictures riding down the conveyor belt. I know the order practically by heart: graduation, graduation, birthday, mountains, baby, baby, new car, bride, bride and groom, house. . . . "I guess so," I say.

"Good," says my sister. "It was getting to be a little much." She puts her tiny brush back in the bottle, capping it. She shows me her nails. They're an odd brown shade. "Cinnamon," she says. "It's an earth color." She looks out into the parking lot. A boy is collecting the abandoned shopping carts, forming a long silver train, which he noses back toward the store. I can tell he is singing by the way his mouth moves.

"That's where we found Keds," my sister says, pointing to the Salvation Army bin.

When I went out to buy cigarettes, Keds would follow me. I hung out down here at night before he died. I was unhappy then, too. That's what no one understands. I named him Keds because he was all white with big black feet and it looked as if he had high-top sneakers on. My mother wanted to name him Bootie. Bootie is a cat's name. It's a dumb name for a dog.

"It's a good thing you weren't here when we found him," my sister says. "You would have gone crazy."

I'm not really listening. It's all nonsense. I'm working on a new problem: Find the value for n such that n plus everything else in your life makes you feel all right. What would n equal? Solve for n.

My lover, Keith, and his daughter, Violet, stood in front of me in the falling snow, clutching flashlights, singing "I'm Dreaming of a White Christmas." They were playing a game they called Christmas Special—a game they apparently played after dark on the day of the first snowfall every year; a game in which I was not asked to participate. I was asked to observe: I was the one-woman audience.

Violet was pretending she was Marie Osmond; Keith was Perry Como—the choice was him or Andy Williams. They had linked arms and were strolling through the snow, in a small circle, singing. I was the camera as well as the audience. Every few minutes Violet looked at me and smiled, but I could tell she wasn't smiling at me: Violet was smiling into the homes of America.

That morning Keith and I had been awakened by screaming in the backyard. I got up and looked out the window. Violet was stamping her feet and waving her arms beneath the clothesline.

"What is it?" asked Keith.

"It's Violet," I said. "She's acting crazy."

"What's new?" said Keith.

"She's dancing or something," I said. "Look. It's snowing."

Keith sat up in bed, swaddling himself in the duvet. "I can't see," he said. "Is she dressed?"

"Yes," I said.

"Then it's O.K.," he said. He lay back down.

I knocked on the window. Violet stopped dancing and looked at me. She motioned, with a pink unmittened hand, for me to join her. "I'm going down," I said. "It's seven-thirty."

I went out and stood on the back steps in my bathrobe and watched Violet dance among the tiny, hesitant flakes.

"What are you doing?" I asked.

"A snow dance," she answered. She didn't look up at me.

I stood there and watched her. She looked a little like an angry bird, stomping and waving.

"If we all do this, it will snow extra hard and we won't have school today," Violet explained. "It will be a snow day."

"It's just begun," I said. It alarmed me that a second grader would already be adept at ways of missing school.

"Come down here," Violet said. "Dance."

I went back inside and watched Violet through the storm door. I didn't join her. I'm not that kind of person. I cannot force myself to participate in meaningless activities, and that's why I don't like children very much. Too much of what they do, like Violet's odd dance, seems purposeless.

Violet sang "O Holy Night" next. Keith was sitting beside me on the steps, with his nose running, as he pointed his beam like a spotlight at Violet's face. She used hers as a microphone and invented her own, terrible, lyrics as she went along. It was actually quite funny, although I knew better than to laugh. Violet finished her song and said, "Well, that's our show for this year. I'd like to thank my special guest stars Perry Como and Britt Ekland and the Osmond Family Singers. Merry Christmas and God Bless."

A car pulled into the driveway, its headlights illuminating the falling snow. Keith's ex-wife, Judith, got out and walked toward us. Violet dropped her flashlight in the snow. It looked pretty there.

Keith shone his flashlight at Judith. She raised her gloved hand to her eyes and squinted, as if she couldn't quite see us. Judith was wearing a coat I had taken off the rack and showed to my friend Marilee the other day in Bradlees. It had fake, diseased-looking fur on its collar and jagged hem. "Who buys coats like this?" I had asked Marilee. When I saw Judith, I felt like going inside and calling Marilee, but I'd see her the next day at work. We run a travel agency together.

Judith is an anthropologist and she's always wearing horrible clothes. Violet tolerates me because I have good taste and occasionally buy her something cute to wear, like her black stirrup pants.

"It's snowing," Judith announced. She picked up Violet's dropped flashlight and shone it across the backyard. Violet was standing under the aluminum clothesline, which looked a little like a dead tree.

"Have I missed the grand finale?" Judith asked. "It's seven o'clock." She pointed the flashlight straight up into the night, and I could see snow falling, in a thin bright column, flake by flake by flake.

* * *

Violet had gone upstairs to find her avocado pit. Ever since I had announced one night, in a momentary lapse of good temper, that I'd be damned if I'd water her pit, Violet had made a great show of carting it back and forth to Judith's on the weekends. This morning I hid it under her bed, so it would take her a while to find it. If she were older, or smarter, she'd accuse me of hiding it, but as it was, she wouldn't. I knew she wouldn't.

Judith and I were sitting at the kitchen table. Keith was shoveling the driveway. When Judith is around, he likes to do helpful things like that, because he never did them when they were married.

"So what's new this week?" Judith asked me. She asks me this every week.

"We went to Violet's concert Wednesday night. Violet was the mouse in 'The Farmer in the Dell.' "

" 'The Farmer in the Dell'!" said Judith. "God, I remember that. What a sick song. Do you think any of them even knew what they were singing about?"

I wasn't sure what Judith meant, so I just shrugged.

"The trouble with these suburban school systems is they're in a time warp. This whole place is in a time warp. I don't know how you can stand it out here. It drove me crazy. I mean, I can see how someone like Keith, someone in his situation, how it could be good for him, but I can't understand how you endure it."

"I have my work," I said.

"Oh, please," said Judith. "Let's not kid ourselves."

Keith came in, stomping his snowy shoes on the floor and rubbing his hands together: the perfect picture of an industrious husband.

"Am I trapped?" asked Judith. "Or did you free me?"

"All clear," said Keith. He took off his coat and began

pouring red wine from a jug into glasses. No one mentioned wine; he was just nervous. Keith doesn't drink
anymore but he thinks it's important for him to serve
drinks to other people. He's always making someone else
a drink now.

Judith lit a cigarette and said, "I got the grant." There
had been a lot of talk about this grant: Judith talked about
it, Keith talked about it, even Violet talked about it. It all
involved Belize and a dig next summer and should Judith
take Violet? I stayed out of it. I was practicing writing my
name backward on a napkin with a red Flair pen. Backward, I wrote a little like Violet.

"Congratulations," said Keith. He placed a glass of
wine in front of Judith, and one on my napkin. The letters
of my name dissolved. There was an awkward silence that
I enjoyed and contributed to: I didn't say anything.

"The dates still aren't settled," said Judith. "But I would
like to take Violet. I mean, I think it's an opportunity we
shouldn't pass up."

Judith is always claiming that she wants to see more of
Violet. Violet goes to school out here and stays with
Judith in the city on the weekends. Judith is always
"looking at" schools in the city for Violet to attend, always talking about taking Violet to Belize with her. In the
end Violet won't go. Mark my words.

"I agree," Keith said.

"I can't find it," Violet yelled down the stairs.

"Look under your bed," I yelled back up. "I think I saw
it there this morning." I smiled at Judith, proud of this
small victory: I had found Violet's avocado pit.

I met Keith in Bloomingdale's about this same time two
years ago. He was one of the guys who try to spray you

with perfume—one of those unnervingly beautiful men: slim-hipped, full-lipped. I held out my wrist, but instead Keith sprayed my neck, leaning towards me and putting a finger on the moist, fragrant spot. He was reflected in all those horrible mirrors, and I remember I felt so much in love so suddenly that I had trouble really seeing him. He seemed to stand there forever with his finger on my warm neck. I didn't buy any perfume, but I went back the next day. On the third day, he quit, but by then he had my phone number.

That happened right after a play he wrote closed. It was Off Off Broadway—for four days. It opened on Thursday and closed after the matinee on Sunday. In the bedroom, there's a plant he was given by the cast after the last performance. He's very proud of it and won't let me water it. It's one of those plants that bloom just once a year, at Easter: flame-like orange flowers that hang for a few days, then fall, and have to be vacuumed up, because they're poisonous. If the cat eats them, she'll die.

After Judith and Violet left, Keith and I went out to dinner. We always do on Friday nights. We used to go to the Willow River Tavern, but lately we've been going to Howard Johnson's, because of the money; since Keith stopped his odd jobs things have gotten tight. Supposedly he's writing a play about hostages in a department store, but I've yet to read any of it. I never saw his first play, and he won't let me read that, either.

Keith had originally suggested HoJo's because Friday was fish fry night, with all the fried clams you can eat for $5.95. Neither of us really likes fried fish, though, so we'd stopped pretending to be there for the special. I ordered a bacon cheeseburger, and Keith had beef Stroganoff. Our waitress was one of my customers; I'd sent her to Fiji and Greece. I mentioned this to Keith.

"If Judith takes Violet this summer, maybe we could go away someplace," he said.

"Where?" I asked.

"I don't know," Keith said. "Anywhere. We've never taken advantage of all your freebies. We could really do some traveling."

This was just talk. We won't travel. Keith only leaves the house on Tuesday mornings, when he's the writer-in-residence at the Wopford Junior High School. Sometimes I think he has that phobia that afflicts housewives.

"Well, let's wait and see before we make any plans," I said.

"It was just a thought," Keith said. "Wouldn't a beer taste good with that?"

"No," I said. "Not after the wine." After a second I said, "And I wish you wouldn't do that."

"Do what?"

"Encourage me to drink. If I want a drink, I'll have one."

"Oh," said Keith. "I'm sorry. It's part of the therapy. A lot of people are reluctant to drink around alcoholics."

"Well, you don't have to do it for me, Keith. I think it's weird."

"I'm sorry," said Keith. "I didn't know it bothered you." He picked up his fork and drew a pattern of four lines in the sauce on his plate, then crossed it with four more.

Our jet-set waitress appeared beside our table. "Are you done with that?" she asked Keith.

Keith looked at his plate. "Yes," he said. "I'm done."

On the way out he bought a pistachio ice cream cone. We sat in the cab of the pickup truck while Keith ate it.

It was still snowing. Keith likes to eat ice cream outside, in winter. In the summer it melts too quickly for him, and he gets upset. In winter, there's no pressure involved.

"He has a key to turn it off," I said. We had just watched the eleven o'clock news, and we were talking about the man with the artificial heart. I was lying in bed watching Keith shave. There's a sink in the bedroom. It's an old house, and our bedroom was originally the sickroom. It was Keith's grandmother's house.

"I know," Keith said. He smiled at me in the mirror. One side of his face was still covered with lather. He had his shirt off and his thin back sloped into his pajama bottoms. Keith always shaves before going to bed. I think this is odd. I had understood that men shave in the morning. Keith's face is always smooth when we make love. He smells of aftershave.

Keith finished shaving and put his pajama top on. I watched him from the bed. He knew I was watching. He knew I loved him. I felt as if I'd forgotten to let in the dog, but we don't have a dog. What was it I'd forgotten to do?

"If he wants to die he has a key to turn it off," I said.

"What if he loses the key?" Keith asked.

"He has another," I said. "I'm sure. Or his wife has one."

"Is he married?"

"I think so."

"Imagine being married to someone with an artificial heart," Keith said. He stood by the window, watching the snow.

"Has it stopped yet?" I asked.

"I think so," Keith said. "It's blowing." He sat on the edge of the bed. I touched him with my foot.

"Do you know what Violet told me?" I asked.

"What?" Keith lay down on the bed, the small of his back arched over my ankles, staring at the ceiling.

"She told me that every Saturday night she and Judith watch 'The Love Boat.' And that Judith cries—she cries every week. Violet didn't understand."

"Didn't understand what?"

"Why Judith cries. She said she pretends not to notice."

For a minute Keith didn't say anything. For a minute I thought I might have fallen asleep. Then Keith said, "Why did you tell me that?"

I thought for a moment, because I wasn't sure. "I don't know," I said.

"Just relax," Keith said. "I love you."

O.K., so he really might love me, I told myself. Everything might really be O.K. I tried to get a sense of myself in bed, with Keith lying across my ankles and the snow blowing outside. But I couldn't feel it. It would all have been O.K. if I could have felt it, but I couldn't. I could have been anywhere. I could have been in Judith's apartment, watching "The Love Boat."

The problem was everyone had these rituals. Keith with his shaving at night and pushups in the morning and tomato juice before dinner and odd jobs, and Judith with her classes every Monday and Wednesday and Friday and her perfectly planned weekends with Violet, and even Violet with her dancing like a pagan at the first scent of snow, her traveling avocado, her seasonal games with Keith. They all had these things that placed them, that kept them connected. I tried to think of what I did; if I celebrated anything or washed my hair in some particular way that had beauty or meaning. I couldn't remember how, exactly, I washed my hair.

"I want more rituals in my life," I said.

"What do you mean by rituals?" Keith asked. He got into bed beside me.

"Things you do over and over. That give meaning to your life. You know—rituals."

"You have rituals," Keith said. "Everyone does."

"What are they?" I asked.

"We go out to dinner every Friday," he suggested.

"I was looking for something a little more meaningful than that."

Keith thought for a second. So did I. I remembered how after Keith quit his job perfuming at Bloomingdale's, he got another job. He helped dress windows at Bergdorf's. I know because I saw him there one night, a few nights after we had slept together for the first time. I walked past the window, and he was inside fastening a fishbowl onto the opened, outstretched palm of a mannequin wearing a black fur coat over a bathing suit. I knocked on the window, and Keith looked up. He smiled but he didn't seem to recognize me. I tried to speak through the glass, but I couldn't. There were two black fish swimming in the fishbowl, and the mannequin was bald.

"I don't know your rituals," Keith finally said. "Only you know them. Rituals are secrets."

I wanted to say, "But I know yours." But I didn't say it, because I suddenly had a sense of that being the moment I could change my life if I really wanted to. I could have run out of the house, into the snow, stood under the clothesline and waited for Keith to come out and promise to marry me, or love me forever. Or promise me something.

Only I was afraid to change my life, because I didn't expect Keith to marry me, or even love me forever. Keith had his last drink in the restaurant on the top of the World Trade Center. Afterward, we went over to the other tower and stood on the observation deck, and Keith promised me that if he stayed sober for two years we would get married. But he was drunk then, and he's never mentioned it again. I think he's forgotten about it.

I haven't. I remember perfectly. Lying in bed beside him, I could still picture it—I could even feel it: Keith and I standing together, the lights below us, the wind in our hair, and in all the clouds around us, the snow just beginning to form, collecting itself, waiting to fall.

Maureen, the new receptionist, told me I had a call on 2, but when I picked up 2 it was Mrs. LaRossa, wanting to know if Kenny had come back from lunch. I told her no, and that I would have him call when he did. Then I picked up 3, which was also blinking. "Hello?" I said.

"Patrick? This is me." It was my friend Alison.

"Hi," I said. "What's happening?"

"Well," said Alison, "it depends what you're doing this weekend. What are you doing this weekend?"

"Nothing," I said.

"Then do you want to come up to Maine with me? I have to visit my mother."

"How is she?" I asked.

"Not too good. That's why I'm going." Alison's mother had some disease. She had been dying, on and off, for years.

"Oh," I said. "That's too bad."

"Can you come? I'm driving up Friday night after work." Alison worked as a projectionist in a movie theater in Cambridge.

"I guess so," I said. "Sure."

"That's great," said Alison. "I really appreciate it. I hate going up there alone. I can't deal with it."

"What time are you leaving?"

"Oh," said Alison. "About midnight. The last show is at ten."

"What is it?"

"My Fair Lady," Alison said. "If you can believe it."

The first time I met Alison's mother I didn't know that she was sick, or that she was dying, although in fact she was.

Alison and I went to college together in Maine, and Mrs. Arbinger, Alison's mother, used to come visit. She'd drive up in her champagne-colored Peugeot and take us out to dinner—Alison and her roommate and anyone else who happened to be around. Since I lived in the same suite, I was usually invited.

The first time I began to realize that Mrs. Arbinger was ill was at graduation. It was held outside, and after it was over I was enduring the photographic zeal of my parents when Alison appeared, looking for her mother. As the sea of chairs slowly emptied, we saw her sitting alone, making no move to get up. Alison ran over; I followed. Mrs. Arbinger was sitting very still. She had recently had some sort of operation on her throat and had wrapped long silk scarves around it.

"What's wrong?" Alison said, panting, although she had not run far.

Mrs. Arbinger smiled. "Nothing," she said. "I just can't stand up. If I stand up I know I'll fall over. I didn't want to make a scene."

"Oh, God," said Alison.

Mrs. Arbinger looked at me. "Patrick," she said. "Congratulations."

* * *

On Friday night, I came home from work and ate a tuna melt. I drank two beers, then fell asleep. When I woke up, it was nine-thirty and I could still taste the tuna melt. I brushed my teeth, and decided to go to the movies.

It wasn't crowded, and I got a good seat and hung my legs over the chair in front of me. I looked back up at the projection booth and saw Alison threading the first reel. I waved, but she didn't see me.

For some reason I'd gotten *My Fair Lady* mixed up with *Hello, Dolly!* I kept waiting for Eliza Doolittle to come into a restaurant and everyone to go crazy, and it was a while —after the scene at Ascot—until I realized it wasn't going to happen. I watched the rest of the movie feeling a little cheated.

When the lights came up, I went into the lobby and up the secret staircase into the booth. Alison was furiously rewinding one reel on the projector and another on the manual rewind. "You won't believe this," she shouted.

"What?" I said.

"There's a midnight show. I've got to show it again."

"My Fair Lady?" I said. "At midnight?"

"Maybe no one will come. If no one shows up, we can leave."

I looked down into the theater. Ten people had already come in. "There are some fools down there," I said.

"Christ," said Alison. "I hate when they do this to me. Could you wind this? I have to splice the second reel. For the third time tonight."

We started the first reel about ten past twelve. Alison turned the sound off in the projection booth and we watched a silent *My Fair Lady.* Alison, who knew all the words by heart, dubbed for Audrey Hepburn. She was almost as good as Marni Nixon. It was a quarter past three by the time we left Boston in Alison's burgundy Peugeot. The Arbingers buy them by the half dozen, I think. I was going through Alison's extensive collection of tapes, playing the one or two songs I liked from each tape. This meant I was spending most of the time fast-forwarding.

"Can't you play just one tape from beginning to end?" Alison asked. She rolled down her window and flicked her cigarette into the night. I watched the sparks fly away. Judy Collins began singing "Who Knows Where the Time Goes?" and it sounded perfect, so I didn't bother to respond.

"Actually," Alison said, rolling up her window, "I have to tell you something."

"What?"

Alison turned the tape down a notch and hung her wrist over the steering wheel. She was going seventy-five. "You're here under false pretenses."

"What? Where?"

"Here," Alison said. "With me. Going to Maine."

"What's false about them?"

Alison looked over at me, then looked back out at the road. "Well, you're my fiancé. We're engaged, and we're getting married in the spring. My mother wants to see you one more time before she dies. She's dying. That's the only reason why I'm subjecting you to this."

"Why?" I asked. "Why did you tell her we were engaged?"

"I don't know. I forget how it all started. For a while she's had this thing about me—about how important it is for me to be married and happy and pregnant and all before she dies. It started very subtly, but as she's got sicker she's kind of latched onto the idea. She wouldn't give it up. And she's always, always liked you—right from the start. She always asks about you, and since we were together at school—at least whenever she came up —it was easy to invent a romance."

"But how did we get engaged?"

"God, it's been going on for so long. If you knew, you would kill me. I mean, you would. I've been awful. We live together in Boston. We're getting married in June, in Maine. I'm wearing my mother's wedding dress." Alison paused. I didn't say anything. "I'm sorry," she said.

I couldn't think what to say. Alison slowed down and pulled over onto the shoulder. The highway was deserted. No cars passed us. It was dark. Judy Collins was singing the whale song. "You don't have to do this," Alison said. "We can turn around."

Alison had always referred to the house in Maine as the Abbey, but it didn't look like one. It looked like a picture I remember of the House of the Seven Gables in a Classics comic book I read in sixth grade: it was all peaky roofs and thin, arched windows.

I didn't really get a good look at it Friday night. I had fallen asleep, and I woke up in the garage. We were parked between two sleeping Peugeots.

"We're here," Alison said.

"What time is it?"

Alison flicked the keys so that the dashboard lights went back on. The digital clock read 5:15. "In a while the sun will come up," she said. "It's just starting to get light."

"Aren't you tired?" I asked.

"No," said Alison.

Upstairs, there was a long hall of closed doors. Alison opened one. "You can sleep in here," she said. "There's a bathroom attached. Sleep as late as you want."

If I had been more awake, I would have asked her what the plan was, but I just nodded. Alison smiled and closed the door.

There was a huge bed in the middle of the room. It looked like a canopy bed, except it had no canopy—just tall posts that ended in carved pineapples. The blankets had been turned back.

I undressed and got into the bed. I thought I would fall asleep right away, but I couldn't. Every time I closed my eyes, I could see Audrey Hepburn running around in her nightgown, singing "I Could Have Danced All Night." It was something about the bed. I got out and sat in a leather chair. Outside the leaded-glass windows, trees appeared.

When I woke up I was back in the bed. I couldn't remember moving. Someone was knocking on the door.

"Yes?" I said.

"Are you decent?" a woman's voice called.

It sounded as if it might have been a moral question, but I figured it wasn't. "Yes," I said. "Come in."

The door opened, and a middle-aged woman stood there in a dress and high heels. "Patrick?" she said. "I'm Mrs. Hawks, Alison's aunt. I just wanted you to know that breakfast is about to be taken away, so if you're hungry you should come down."

She disappeared but left the door open. I thought I could still hear her in the hall, and I tried to figure out how to get out of the bed without being seen in my underwear. Finally, I kind of rolled out and crawled into the bathroom.

When I came downstairs—it took me a while to find the stairs—Mrs. Hawks was standing in the front hall going through mail. "You might find something nourishing in the dining room," she said, pointing across the hall.

"Is Alison up?" I asked.

"Goodness, yes. She's in with her mother."

I was eating a charred apple when Alison came into the dining room. She was wearing a kilt and a white blouse with ruffles. It looked a little like a national costume. "Why are you dressed like that?" I asked.

"My mother ordered them for me. I was just trying them on."

"Are they part of your trousseau?" I asked.

"Will you shut up," Alison said. "Now, you have a choice."

"I thought we decided to go through with it."

"No, not the wedding story," Alison said. "The dentist."

"I have to go to the dentist?"

"No. I do. Do you want to come? That's your choice. Do you want to come?"

"What's the alternative?" I asked.

"Staying here," said Alison.

The dentist was really the dentist's daughter. He had died, and she had inherited his practice. The office was in the garage of their house, and while Alison visited with the dentist I sat in the living room. The dentist's mother was the receptionist. She got me a cup of coffee. "Are you a friend of Alison's?" she asked.

"Yes," I said. "We went to school together."

"I hear Alison's engaged."

"Did you? I thought it was a secret."

"Oh," she said. "Well, Mrs. Hawks told me. She had her gums scraped. She didn't say it was a secret."

"It is," I said.

"Are you the lucky man?"

"No," I said.

"Alison's a nice girl. It's just too bad she can't find something to do with her life. Patty's always known she wanted to be a dentist. It's easier for the girls who are like that, I suppose. Is Alison still working in that movie house?"

"Yes. She's the manager now," I lied.

"Is she really? Well, good for her." The phone rang and the woman answered it.

A few minutes later, Alison came out of the garage looking angry. "Let's get out of here," she said.

"Don't you have to pay?"

"No," said Alison. "This is Maine. They bill me."

Once we had turned the corner and the dentist's house had disappeared Alison said, "I never did like her. She told me I had gum disease. I don't have gum disease. My gums are fine. She just wants to get back at me."

"For what?"

"I don't know," Alison said. "For being popular, I suppose. Patty was kind of a drip in high school."

"Maybe you do have gum disease. Do you floss?"

"Patrick," Alison said. "Lay off."

After a few minutes Alison seemed to relax. At least we slowed down a little.

"How's your mother?" I asked.

"She seems O.K.," Alison said. "It's hard to tell."

"Why isn't she in a hospital?"

"She's a Christian Scientist. Plus she's past that point."

"What point?"

"The point where you stay at the hospital. She'd have been sent home. We have a special nurse there." Alison pulled into the parking lot of a supermarket. "Do you want to get some real food? The macrobiotic diet at the Abbey is enough to kill you."

"Is that what it is? I think I had a baked apple for breakfast."

Alison opened her door. "Wait till you see lunch."

We went into the supermarket and bought onion bagels, Doritos, Pepperidge Farm cookies, and a six-pack of Busch beer.

When we got back in the car, Alison said, "She wants to see you this afternoon. She's usually pretty good in the afternoon, but you don't have to go. I can say you went fishing."

"It's raining," I said.

"Isn't that when people fish?"

"I'll see her," I said. "I might as well."

"Then there's just one thing I have to tell you."

"What?"

"Well, in addition to marrying me, you're also going to law school."

"Law school! Alison, that's cruel." I had applied and been denied admission to almost every decent law school in the eastern United States.

"Well, it made my mother very happy," she said. "For you and for me."

"Where am I going?"

"BU," said Alison. "I thought Harvard was stretching it."

After lunch (brown rice, seaweed, and beet juice) Alison and I went up to see Mrs. Arbinger. She lay in a big bed like the one I had slept in the night before, only this one had a canopy. Her face was very thin and pale, but her eyes were bright. She had so much lipstick on that it looked as if her mouth had come off and been clumsily reattached. The nurse, who was dressed in a caftan, sat on a window seat, knitting. Alison sat on the bed, and I stood beside it.

Mrs. Arbinger looked around at all of us for a moment. "It's like a party," she said. No one answered. "Look what I found," she continued, undaunted. "My wedding album." She indicated a white book on the bed beside her. She opened the album to a picture of her and Mr. Arbinger cutting a many-tiered wedding cake. They stood side by side, clasping hands on a cake knife that was pointed at the marzipan bride and groom. They were divorced soon after Alison was born. Mr. Arbinger lived in Italy now. I'd never met him. Mrs. Arbinger turned the page to a picture of her standing at the top of a curved staircase in her wedding gown, her bouquet dripping vines over the bannister.

"I was a beautiful bride," Mrs. Arbinger said, more to the picture than to any of us. She closed the book. "You'll be beautiful, too," she said to Alison. "I hope the dress fits. Have you tried it on?"

"Not yet," said Alison.

"You must. It will have to be altered. That kind of dress must fit perfectly; otherwise it looks cheap."

"Let's not talk about the wedding," Alison said. "It makes me nervous." She stood up. As if on cue, the nurse stopped her knitting and stood up, too.

"Do you think I could talk to Patrick alone?" Mrs. Arbinger said to no one in particular.

"I was just going down to get your juice," the nurse said.

"I'll come, too," said Alison. They both left.

Mrs. Arbinger waited a moment. I thought she had

forgotten about me. Then she patted the bed beside her. Her fingers were very thin and her rings twisted around below her knuckles. "Sit down," she said. "Please."

The comforter was so puffy and Mrs. Arbinger was so thin that I couldn't really tell where her body began. I perched on the foot of the bed, and Mrs. Arbinger patted a spot nearer to her. The patting seemed to exhaust her. "A little closer," she said.

I moved up the bed. She took one of my hands in hers. For a moment I thought she was going to read my palm, but she just looked at it, then put it back on the bed and patted it. She smiled at me. I noticed that her teeth were very white. They looked like the only healthy part of her left. I wondered if they were dentures.

"It's so nice to see you," Mrs. Arbinger said. "It was nice of you to come up."

I just nodded.

"I'm sorry for cloistering you like this but I wanted to tell you how happy I am about you and Alison. I've always been fond of you, and I'm so pleased. I won't say any more because I don't want to embarrass you."

"I'm happy, too," I said, although it didn't sound like my voice. "Thank you."

Mrs. Arbinger looked toward the window. "Will you do me a favor?" she asked.

"Of course," I said.

"Will you look out the window? I'm not allowed out of bed and I miss seeing outside."

I got off the bed and went over to the window. There was a pond at the back of the house, and behind that a field with a horse in it, and behind that some woods.

"Can you see the pond?" Mrs. Arbinger asked.

"Yes," I said.

"Are there any geese in it?"

"No," I said.

"Oh," she said. "There will be. Are the leaves pretty?"

"Yes."

"Do you mind doing this?"

"No," I said.

"It's just that I like to picture it in my head and want to get it right. What color are the leaves?"

"Mostly yellow," I said. "Some red. It's raining."

She waited a moment before she asked the next question. "Do you and Alison really want to get married?" she asked, quietly.

I looked over at her. I had the feeling she had been watching me at the window and had turned away; she gazed up at the white tented canopy. "What?" I said.

"Forgive me if I'm being rude," she said, still not looking at me. "I just want to make sure, and I can't ask Alison."

"Sure of what?" I said.

"I don't want you to do this just for me," she said. "I know you're in love, but I also know people wait longer to get married nowadays. I just don't want you to rush into this to make me happy. You needn't do that."

I think that if she had continued to look at the canopy I would have answered differently. But she didn't. She turned her small, wrecked face toward me and smiled.

"Oh, no," I said. "We want very much to get married."

We sat there for a moment. I thought there were tears in Mrs. Arbinger's eyes, but I wasn't sure, because there seemed to be tears in my own.

The nurse came in, carrying a small silver tray. On it was a glass of beet juice.

* * *

When I went downstairs it had stopped raining. Alison and I went for a walk. We fed carrots to the fat white horse in the field, and then followed a gravel path into the woods. The sun was setting as we walked into the far side of the field an hour later, and the sight of the white horse completely disoriented me. I had thought we were walking deeper and deeper into the woods, but it was an illusion. The straight path had curved, imperceptibly, all along. As we walked around the pond, we heard a noise behind us, and when we looked back we saw a shaking V of geese appear. They descended and skidded into the pond, then collected themselves and swam over to the grassy bank. They lowered themselves into the shadows. We stood and watched until they had disappeared, until even the water in the pond had regained its composure.

Alison didn't ask me what her mother and I had talked about. I didn't tell her.

Alison and I left the Abbey the next morning before anyone else was awake. She dropped me at my apartment and drove away, and I didn't see her for a couple of months, until we met at a New Year's Eve party in Cambridge. We were sitting together on the edge of a platform bed, but it was hard to talk. The room was way too crowded, and people were dancing behind us on the bed.

"Come on," Alison shouted. "Let's go someplace quieter."

I followed her into the bathroom. Alison sat on the rim of the bathtub, which was filled with ice and champagne bottles. No two bottles looked alike, and the idea of their being purchased separately all over town and then dumped together in the bathtub appealed to me.

"I have something to tell you," Alison said. "I should have told you before."

"What?" I said.

"My mother died."

"Oh," I said, shocked. I had thought Mrs. Arbinger would be around for a long time. "When?"

"Before Christmas. December fifteenth."

"I'm sorry," I said. Someone knocked on the door. "Go away!" I shouted.

Alison had her fingers in the icy water, pushing the bottles down and then watching them pop back up.

"Why didn't you tell me sooner?" I asked.

"I don't know," Alison said. "I hate this whole episode in my life. I wanted to forget all about it. I'm seeing a therapist, if you can believe it. She thinks I was manipulated by my mother's illness into promising things I feel guilty about not doing now."

"You mean like the wedding?"

"Yes," said Alison.

"Maybe we should get engaged, and get married, just the way we planned."

"And then what?"

"Live happily ever after," I said. "Or get divorced." Alison smiled.

"Why did you pick me?" I asked.

"What?" She bobbed another bottle.

"Why did you ask me to do that?"

"Because you're sweet," Alison said.

"Oh," I said. "So you didn't really want to get married?"

Alison looked at me. "Oh, Patrick," she said. "Did you really think I did?"

"No," I said. I shook my head. "Of course not."

"Good," said Alison. "I don't want to have to feel guilty about that, too." She stood up, then bent over and took a bottle of champagne from its bath. "Let's drink this now," she said. "I have to leave at eleven-thirty. I'm projecting the special midnight show."

"What movie is it?" I asked.

"Bringing Up Baby," Alison said.

She leaned over and kissed my cheek and touched my neck. Her hand was cold and wet. She began to uncork the champagne bottle. I closed my eyes. I hate waiting for things to explode.